"Tell me, Emi̶̶ ̶̶ ̶̶ ̶̶ ̶̶ ̶̶ ̶̶ ̶̶ ̶̶ ̶̶ about ma̶̶̶r̶̶̶r̶̶̶i̶̶̶a̶̶̶g̶̶̶e̶̶̶"

Ben asked, taking her hand and lacing her fingers with his.

"Marriage? I don't know, I've never thought about it."

"Come on," he prompted. "Everyone thinks about it at one time or another. I need some insight into the female mind. What would you say if a man, me for example, asked you to marry him?"

"I...I don't know," Emily said. His words threw her into confusion. The way he leaned forward across the table, looking so deeply into her eyes, she almost thought he really was asking her to marry him. Which of course he wasn't. But if he was...how could she say no? How could anyone say no? She tried to look away, afraid he'd read her thoughts, afraid he could see the love she'd been hiding for three years.

Oh, Lord, how was she ever going to get through this evening?

Dear Reader,

September's stellar selections beautifully exemplify Silhouette Romance's commitment to publish strong, emotional love stories that touch every woman's heart. In *The Baby Bond*, Lilian Darcy pens the poignant tale of a surrogate mom who discovers the father knew nothing of his impending daddyhood! His demand: a marriage of convenience to protect their BUNDLES OF JOY....

Carol Grace pairs a sheik with his plain-Jane secretary in a marriage meant to satisfy family requirements. But the oil tycoon's shocked to learn that being *Married to the Sheik* is his VIRGIN BRIDE's secret desire.... FOR THE CHILDREN, Diana Whitney's miniseries that launched in Special Edition in August 1999—and returns to that series in October 1999—crosses into Silhouette Romance with *A Dad of His Own*, the touching story of a man, mistaken for a boy's father, who ultimately realizes that mother and child are exactly what he needs.

Laura Anthony explores the lighter side of love in *The Twenty-Four-Hour Groom*, in which a pretend marriage between a lawman and his neighbor kindles some very real feelings. WITH THESE RINGS, Patricia Thayer's Special Edition/Romance cross-line miniseries, moves into Romance with *Her Surprise Family*, with a woman who longs for a husband and home and unexpectedly finds both. And in *A Man Worth Marrying*, beloved author Phyllis Halldorson shows the touching romance between a virginal schoolteacher and a much older single dad.

Treasure this month's offerings—and keep coming back to Romance for more compelling love stories!

Enjoy,

Mary-Theresa Hussey

Mary-Theresa Hussey
Senior Editor

Please address questions and book requests to:
Silhouette Reader Service
U.S.: 3010 Walden Ave., P.O. Box 1325, Buffalo, NY 14269
Canadian: P.O. Box 609, Fort Erie, Ont. L2A 5X3

VIRGIN BRIDES

MARRIED TO THE SHEIK

Carol Grace

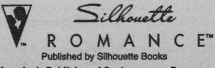

Silhouette
ROMANCE™
Published by Silhouette Books
America's Publisher of Contemporary Romance

SILHOUETTE BOOKS

ISBN 0-373-19391-2

MARRIED TO THE SHEIK

Copyright © 1999 by Carol Culver

Visit us at www.romance.net

Printed in U.S.A.

Books by Carol Grace

Silhouette Romance

Make Room for Nanny #690
A Taste of Heaven #751
Home Is Where the Heart Is #882
Mail-Order Male #955
The Lady Wore Spurs #1010
*Lonely Millionaire #1057
*Almost a Husband #1105
*Almost Married #1142
The Rancher and the Lost Bride #1153
#Granted: Big Sky Groom #1277
#Granted: Wild West Bride #1303
#Granted: A Family for Baby #1345
Married to the Sheik #1391

*Miramar Inn
#Best-Kept Wishes

Silhouette Desire

Wife for a Night #1118
The Heiress Inherits a Cowboy #1145
Expecting... #1205

CAROL GRACE

has always been interested in travel and living abroad. She spent her junior year in college in France and toured the world working on the hospital ship *HOPE*. She and her husband spent the first year and a half of their marriage in Iran, where they both taught English. Then, with their toddler daughter, they lived in Algeria for two years.

Carol says that writing is another way of making her life exciting. Her office is her mountaintop home, which overlooks the Pacific Ocean and which she shares with her inventor husband, their daughter, who just graduated college, and their teenage son.

Dear Reader,

The VIRGIN BRIDE. Who is she? She's the woman in white coming down the aisle with a veil over her face. Her hands are shaky, her heart is pounding, her eyes are misty. The music swells. All heads turn to watch her, but she has eyes only for him. The man who's waiting for her at the altar. Just as she's been waiting for him— all her life. The man of her dreams. Her first love. Her only love.

I know exactly how she feels. Though I was married in a redwood forest under a canopy of trees with only our families in attendance, I, too, wore a white dress. My heart pounded, my hands shook and my eyes filled with happy tears as I married the man of my dreams, a man I'd first met eleven years before. Some years later we built a house in that same forest, where we live today with our two children.

The VIRGIN BRIDE. Wherever she is, whatever she wears, whoever she marries, she's on the brink of a new beginning. The awakening of her passionate self. She knows she's made the right decision. To discover the wonders of physical love with her hero, her lover, her husband.

Sincerely,

Carol Grace

Chapter One

When Sheik Ben Ali was away from his San Francisco office, things were calm, peaceful, relaxed and yes, down-right boring. At least that was the opinion of his super-efficient administrative assistant, Emily Claybourne. Just the anticipation of his return set the top floor of the building that housed his booming oil conglomerate humming and yes, her heart pounding, too.

He'd called from the airport. He was on his way. Word traveled fast through the U.S. headquarters of Oil International.

"He's at the airport."

"Look busy. He's on his way."

Emily's hands shook as she arranged a bouquet of hybrid tea roses for his desk. It was ridiculous. There was nothing to be nervous about. She'd worked for him for three years, and he'd never been anything but appreciative of her efforts. Complimented her on work well done and given her generous raises before she even asked.

Then why did her pulse quicken at the sound of his voice

on the phone? Why did she feel faint when she looked out the window and saw him get out of his limo nineteen floors below? She stepped back from the window, pressed her hands against her temples. As if she didn't know the answer to those questions! She knew perfectly well, she'd known forever, that she was madly, hopelessly in love with her boss.

Everyone knows that any woman who falls in love with her boss is certifiably crazy, but when her boss is a real, honest-to-God sheik from an oil-rich kingdom with more money than he knows what to do with, she ought to be taken straight to the loony bin. Add the fact that Ben, as he insisted she call him, had the smoldering, movie-star good looks of an Antonio Banderas, and you had a real nutcase on your hands.

But Emily hid it well. No one would ever guess that under her tailored suits and sensible mid-heel shoes, behind her rimless glasses, her straight hair pulled back behind her ears, there was a passionate soul longing to escape.

At nine thirty-five he burst in the door and slammed it behind him. "Emily, get me the rector at St. Mark's Church on the phone and then the manager of the Fairmont Hotel." Sheik Ben Ali didn't waste much time on formalities. Not when he had something on his mind.

"Then I want a printout of every woman I've dated in the past two years, with their marital status updated. What is it, what are you staring at?" he asked, his forehead creased in a frown.

"Nothing," she said. "I just wondered..."

"You just wondered what was going on," he said, tossing his briefcase on the lacquered Chinese chest that served as a coffee table. "What's going on is I'm getting married."

Emily knocked the vase over and spilled water all over

his desk. He didn't notice. Her hands shaking, she dabbed ineffectually at the pool of water with her handkerchief.

"Congratulations," she said, her voice trembling just slightly. "Who is the...the lucky girl, I mean woman?"

"I have no idea," he said blandly. "But it's about time, wouldn't you say?"

She didn't say anything; she just stood like a statue made of stone. It was times like this she wished she was made of stone. Then she wouldn't feel. No pain, no jealousy, nothing. Ben getting married. She'd known it would happen sooner or later, but...but...not now.

When she didn't answer, he shot a brief glance in her direction. "You're acting strange today. You've hardly said a word since I got back. What's wrong with you? You look pale. Are you sick? Sit down," he ordered.

Obediently she sat in the straight-backed Eames chair in front of his desk and stared straight ahead without seeing anything.

"I guess *you* wouldn't say it was about time," he continued. "But my father did. In no uncertain terms. 'Son, you're approaching thirty-five,'" Ben said, lowering his voice in an accurate imitation of the old sheik. "'And you know what that means. If you haven't found a bride by October, I'll have to find one for you.'"

Ben went to the window, his hands stuffed in the pockets of his Italian-made suit, pensively looking out at the Golden Gate Bridge. Suddenly he turned to face Emily.

"Do you know what he means?" he demanded.

Tongue-tied, she shook her head.

"It means he's going to line up some cousin twice removed for me, whose face I won't see until the wedding day for a good reason, and whose extended family would all move in with me tomorrow. So right now we have to drop everything—the petroleum company merger, the expansion into Indonesia, the buyout of the North Slope. Until we find me a wife.''

''We?'' she said weakly.

''Yes, we,'' he said impatiently. ''We as in you and I. I've never done anything important without you, and I'm not going to start now. You're organized, efficient, knowledgeable, and you know what I want.''

''I do?''

''Someone special.''

''Tall, short, beautiful, talented, smart?'' she asked, stalling for time. She'd do anything for Ben, but she wouldn't, she couldn't, help him find a wife.

He shook his head. ''None of those things count. Of course it would be nice... No, it doesn't matter. What I want is a bright, savvy woman who knows what's what, and who wants what I want. A marriage of convenience.''

Emily crossed and uncrossed her legs. Her stomach was churning as she worked up the nerve to tell him she couldn't do it. Worry lines etched themselves between her eyebrows. ''I appreciate your confidence in me, and I'm flattered you think I can help, but, Ben, I...I can't do this,'' she said.

''What is it you want, a raise, more vacation time, shorter hours?''

''No, that's not it. I just don't know how to go about finding a...a wife.'' Sadly, she knew even less about finding a husband.

''Do you think I do?'' he asked, leaning against his desk and rolling up the sleeves of his tailored white shirt. ''But how hard can it be?''

After two weeks without his virile, masculine presence, without his deep voice booming from behind closed doors, his demands, his rich laughter, Emily was having an attack of overwhelm. Overwhelmed by the sight of his sun-bronzed arms covered with fine black hairs, overwhelmed by his height, the width of his shoulders, his deep dark eyes, his...his...

"It's not about love, you know," he said, interrupting her reverie. "Which makes everything easier. It's about money. Something everyone understands. It boils down to paying someone to marry me. It's not going to be forever, you know. After a year we get a quiet divorce, she gets a large settlement and everybody's happy."

"What about your father?"

"We have a deal. I told him I was willing to give marriage a try. But if it didn't work, I'd have to get a divorce. After mulling it over, he agreed. And I agreed to stay married a year before I call it quits. He seemed happy with that. In fact, he looked downright smug when I left him. He's from the old school, you know. He believes love comes after marriage, not before. He never saw my mother until their wedding day, and I must say they're very happy together."

"Then why don't you..."

"Because I don't want to get married," he said, anticipating her question. "Why should I? I have the pick of the most glamorous and exciting women in town with no obligations and total freedom, I'm the envy of all my married friends. Why would I want to get married?"

Emily shrugged, stifling questions like what about children, what about loneliness and companionship. Instead she said, "But since you are getting married, why don't you try, really try to fall in love and then marry somebody for real? Wouldn't that be simpler and more satisfying?" she asked. "And save you the trouble of getting divorced."

"Emily, you have signs of being a hopeless romantic. Have you ever been in love?" he asked, fixing her with his dark gaze.

Her face turned as pink as the flowers she'd picked from her garden that morning for his office. Never been in love. Not until she walked into the offices of Oil International and took a look at her new boss. Never been in love, never even *made* love.

"I didn't think so," he continued. "Do you know why? It's because there's no such thing as love except in song and story. As for marriage, well I've never tried it, but I have a pretty good idea of what it entails. Oh, I came close once or twice. But either the women were too dependent or too independent. One complained I spent too much time at work. That I had no time for her. Another that she needed her space. Neither was much of a homemaker. Even though I've been in this country since college, in some ways I'm still a traditional man," he admitted. "It seems to me a woman's place—"

"Is in the home," Emily murmured.

He acknowledged her comment with a wry smile. "You don't agree, do you? I understand that. After all, you're a career woman yourself. But it is true that where I come from the wife stays home and the husband goes to work. Was I sad when these relationships fell apart? Not really. Was I heartbroken? Of course not." He rubbed his forehead. "I don't know why I'm telling you all this, except that I want you to understand me, so you'll know why I'm doing this," he said. "Now, are you with me or not, Emily?"

She'd been prepared to say no, and if she hadn't heard the sincerity in his voice, if she hadn't been touched by his need for her help, his willingness to confide in her— But she did hear it and she was touched and she couldn't possibly say no to him. Not when he needed her.

She sighed deeply and got to her feet. "Yes, okay."

He rubbed his hands together and smiled, his teeth

gleaming like a shark's, the way he did when he'd just gotten the best of a competitor in a close deal.

"Good girl," he said, patting her on the shoulder. "You won't regret it. I'll make it up to you."

As Ben watched her go, her hips swaying just slightly under the too-large plain navy-blue suit she wore, he caught a glimpse of long, shapely legs under her skirt, and wondered for the first time in three years what she did when she wasn't in the office. For the life of him he couldn't picture her in anything but a dark suit, couldn't imagine her laughing or dancing or God forbid, making love.

He shook his head to dispel the image. If it weren't for this discussion they'd had about marriage, he never would have thought about it. Never wondered about his super-secretary's life after work. Because of her, he was the envy of all his friends.

"I'd give anything for an assistant like Emily," they said.

"Easygoing, self-effacing, calm in the face of emergency," they enthused. "Loyal and trustworthy."

He'd smile smugly and give her another raise. That's why he was surprised today at her near refusal to help him with this marriage business. She looked downright disapproving. Though he didn't know why. He didn't want to get married, he was perfectly happy playing the field—no commitments, no hard feelings, and best of all, no emotional entanglements. But because of his father and the family custom of marrying on or before the thirty-fifth birthday, he was giving it another try. But just for a year. What was wrong with that?

One thing for sure. He couldn't do it without her. He couldn't do anything without her. Work aside, she'd done all the paperwork on the condo he'd bought on Telegraph Hill, and she'd found the decorator. He'd had to rein her in when she suggested a garden on the penthouse patio; having to take care of plants smacked of responsibility and commitment. But aside from that, her taste was flawless. She seemed to know what he liked before he knew he liked it.

She bought presents for his nieces and nephews back in his country as well as the ones in the U.S. She made reservations at all the best restaurants, kept his dates straight so that he never stood anyone up. She knew more about him than anyone. He couldn't imagine life without her. He couldn't imagine finding a wife without her.

But even with her help it wasn't as easy as he'd imagined. From the list she'd prepared, he made dates with every available woman he knew during the weeks ahead. He wined and dined them and then, just when he was ready to haul our the four-carat ring he'd purchased and propose, he couldn't do it. Why not? He didn't know. He just couldn't imagine being married to any one of them. Even for a year. Even for convenience.

So at the end of three weeks he had no fiancée. He had the huge bauble he'd bought at Tiffany's, but nobody to give it to. As dusk fell over the city, he propped his feet on his desk, he turned down the lamps, leaned back and pensively watched the lights go on all over the Marina. His office door opened and Emily came in with a stack of file folders in her arms.

"Oh," she said, so startled to see him sitting in semi-darkness that she dropped everything on the floor, scattering papers everywhere. "I thought you'd left." She flipped on the lights and bent over to pick up the papers, but he beat her to it. For a man who was brought up by servants to attend his every wish, Ben was amazingly considerate.

On their knees, side by side, they sorted and stacked until

every paper was back in the correct folder. At least she hoped they were. Every time his hand brushed hers or she inhaled his heady masculine aftershave Emily got so rattled she couldn't tell an import license from a purchase order. Or the Mackenzie file from Remsen. She just wished he'd go home and let her do it herself.

By the time he'd restacked the papers and helped her to her feet she was not the same perfectly calm administrative assistant who'd walked in the door a few minutes ago. She was a bundle of nerves, a palpitating heart, a dry mouth and a pair of wobbly knees.

Clutching the folders tightly to her chest, as if she could protect herself from the potent masculine charm he exuded from every pore, she looked at her watch. "What are you doing here? You have a reservation at Paoli's at eight. Did you forget?"

"I didn't forget, but my date did. She forgot she had to go out of town tonight."

"I'm sorry."

"I'm not. There's something wrong with the system or the list. This plan is just not working." He observed her through narrowed eyes. "We have to think of something else."

She glanced at her watch. Not that she had any plans. She just didn't want to spend any more time talking about who Ben was going to marry. Especially not on a Friday night after a difficult week where her boss was in a decidedly bad temper. Now she knew why. He hadn't found Ms. Right yet.

"Now?" she asked.

"Why? Are you busy tonight?"

"No, but..."

"But it's late and you're hungry," he said, finishing her sentence for her. "And so am I. It's impossible to think on an empty stomach.'' Briskly he removed the folders from her arms, his fingers accidentally grazing the edge of her breast under her suit jacket. He didn't notice, but she jumped as if she'd received an electric shock. Tremors ran up and down her spine while he set the files on his desk and went to the closet where he retrieved his navy blazer with the gold buttons.

''We'll discuss this over dinner,'' he said, shoving his arms through the sleeves. ''You and I are going to Paoli's. After a good meal and a few glasses of wine we'll come up with something. A new plan. What do you say?''

Emily licked her dry lips. Did it matter what she said? She was going to an expensive restaurant with her boss. She was going to sit across the white tablecloth and eat and drink by candlelight while they discussed his upcoming marriage. She was expected to come up with a new plan to help him find a wife while her heart pounded, her hands shook and her stomach churned. She couldn't think of anything worse. Except the Chinese water torture.

''I can't,'' she said.

He raised his eyebrows in surprise. No wonder. She never turned him down. No matter what he asked.

''Why not?'' he asked. ''I thought you said you weren't busy. Do you have a date?''

A date? She didn't date. She worked and she grew roses. She grew roses and she was the president of her garden club. That was her life. It was her life and she liked it. ''No, it's not that. I just can't, that's all. I'm out of ideas. I don't know how to help you any more than I have. My mind is a blank.''

''What are you talking about? You're full of ideas. You helped me convince Union Oil to join the consortium. You're the one who suggested I use a multimedia presentation to clinch the deal. You wrote my speech for OPEC last year. You helped me persuade my competition to lower his oil prices. This is the same thing. Only more important. Those were business, this is family. Family is just as important. Maybe more so. Together we can come up with something. We always do.''

She wanted to scream, No, no, not this time. But her vocal chords were frozen solid and wouldn't cooperate. Ben, taking her silence for acceptance, briskly took her arm and led her out of his office and out to her desk. Like a robot, she picked up her purse and her coat, fully intending to find a way out of this predicament before they got to the restaurant. She'd already stupidly said she had no date. But would he have believed her if she said she had? Plain Emily Claybourne, a date? Not likely.

She might plead ill. She could throw up or faint. She could open the car door at a stop sign and jump out. She could... No, she couldn't do anything but hope to get through the evening without falling apart by agreeing with anything and everything he said. Because she was serious when she said she had no ideas.

Once in his vintage Porsche, the one she'd had tuned up for him while he was away, the expensive smell of leather and wool, the heated seats, the soft music from the state-of-the-art sound system, all combined to make her feel cosseted and protected and comfortable and yes, rich.

She gazed out the window as he drove down Montgomery Street, looking at people waiting for a bus at the same corner where she usually waited for the bus. She never drove to work. Parking downtown was too expensive, and she had learned the value of thrift when she was a child, as a reaction to her crazy impractical family.

She looked at the people trying to hail a cab, she looked at the people still at work in the tall office buildings that lined the financial district. She looked anywhere but in the direction of her impossibly rich, incredibly good-looking and terribly sexy boss. Just a glance at his large, capable hands on the steering wheel caused her heart rate to accelerate.

The sight of his royal, imperial profile, his proud, hawk-like nose, his high cheekbones and wide, mobile mouth made her feel faint. She was so close to him she could feel the heat from his body. She was far too close in this compact, high-powered car, a car that reflected his love of beautiful lines, mechanical excellence and outstanding performance. All the traits he wanted in a wife, if he wanted a wife, which he really didn't.

She sighed. After all these years her secret dream of going out with Ben had come true. And how she wished it hadn't. It was not at all the way she'd dreamed it. It was strange and awkward and hazardous to her emotional health. Right now she would have given her right arm to be home watering her roses, checking for aphids and chatting over the back fence with her next-door neighbor and fellow rose grower. She chastised herself for letting this situation happen. For not thinking faster on her feet. For not coming up with a believable excuse.

"I appreciate this," Ben said, maneuvering expertly through the evening traffic. "Your coming on such short notice. I realize you probably have better things to do than work overtime. But I'm desperate. I promised my father, and I have to go through with it. It means a lot to him—this marriage and family business. And I don't go back on my promises."

"I just hope you don't expect me to come up with any answers. If you do, you're going to be disappointed," she murmured.

"When have you ever disappointed me?" he asked.

There was a first time for everything, she thought. A first

time for a pseudo date, a first time to have dinner at Paoli's, where the lights were soft, the walls covered with fine art, the atmosphere rarefied and the maître d' suave.

"Good evening, sir." Robert, the white-jacketed head waiter, had just the right blend of deference. Not too friendly, not too obsequious.

"Sorry to be late, Robert. A slight change in plans," Ben said smoothly.

A slight change in plans and more than a slight change in his date. She was painfully aware of how different she looked from Ben's usual dates. If only she'd had time to change. To make a trip to the hairdresser, to a boutique to pick up a new dress, then have her nails done. As if that was all she needed. She needed a complete makeover, from head to toe, inside and out, if she wanted to compete with the women he usually went out with on Friday nights.

But she didn't. She was his assistant. Not his date. She was there to assist him in coming up with a new idea for finding a mate. If she forgot that for even one minute she was in big trouble.

Ben rested his hand on the small of her back as they followed the head waiter to a quiet booth in the corner. His usual booth. The booth where he plied women with fine wine and rich food and subtle flattery.

She looked around the room at the stylish women in smart little dresses, dripping diamonds and pearls, their hair professionally coiffed, and realized just how far out of her element she was. And she thanked heaven for the semi-darkness of their corner table.

After he'd ordered for both of them and approved the wine the sommelier brought to the table, Ben leaned across the table and gazed into her eyes.

"Tell me something, Emily," he said, his voice as

smooth as the vintage cabernet sauvignon he'd ordered. "How do you feel about marriage?"

"Marriage? I don't know, I never thought about it."

He took her hand and laced her slender fingers through his, and all the breath left her lungs. She only hoped he couldn't tell how much her hands were shaking.

"Come on," he prompted. "Everybody thinks about it at one time or another. I need some insight into the female mind. What would you say if a man, me for example, asked you to marry him?"

"I...I don't know," she said. His words threw her into confusion. She knew this was all part of the process, to help him think things through. But the way he leaned forward across the table, looking so deeply into her eyes, she almost thought he really was asking her to marry him. Which of course he wasn't. But if he was...how could she say no? How could anyone say no? She tried to look away, afraid he'd read her thoughts, afraid he could see the love she'd been hiding for three years.

He was still waiting for her answer. But the longer he waited and the longer he gazed into her eyes, the harder it was for her to think. Of all times when she needed to be alert and aware, her brain had gone AWOL. It could have been the wine, though she'd only had one sip. It was more likely the fact that Ben was still holding her hand. That he'd begun to slowly caress her palm with his thumb. A sensuous motion, which caused an unfamiliar and disturbing throbbing somewhere deep in her womb. If this was his typical modus operandi, how could anyone turn him down? They couldn't. All he had to do was ask. Oh, Lord, how was she ever going to get through this evening?

Just when she thought she'd have to plead a sick headache, the waiter arrived at their table with their salad. Emily withdrew her hand from Ben's grip and regained a small part of her composure.

But after some small talk and after the salad plates had been cleared, Ben turned his dark gaze on her again. "Let me put it another way. You're still single at…what… twenty-seven? What are you holding out for? What do you want?"

"Just what everyone wants. True love," she said. There, that ought to stop this line of inquiry. He could offer a woman a great deal. But not that. Not true love.

"True love," Ben repeated, shaking his head. "There's no such thing, Emily. I hate to disillusion you, but it doesn't exist. Not in real life."

She wanted to tell him he was wrong. That it did exist, like a dormant rosebush, just waiting to bloom with the proper care. But how could she, without giving away her secret?

"What does exist," Ben continued, "is respect. Mutual respect and mutual needs. For example, what do you need?"

She waited until the waiter had brought their savory, golden-brown crab cakes before she spoke.

"I don't need anything," she said primly. After all, she had her job, her garden club, a car and a wonderful little bungalow in the avenues where she could garden to her heart's content.

Ben drummed his knuckles on the white tablecloth. "Let me put it another way," he said. "What do you *want*, then?"

"Well…"

"Come on, let's have it," he said with a trace of impatience. "Diamonds, a sports car, a trip to Tahiti?"

She paused.

"A greenhouse," she said at last. "That's what I'm saving for. A greenhouse with an automatic watering system and climate control. Big enough for rugosas and sweetbrier roses and warm enough to grow them year-round.''

''Now we're making progress,'' he said, rubbing his hands together. ''If I bought you a greenhouse, plus a lump-sum payment at the end of the year, would you marry me?''

She almost choked on a sprig of parsley. The longing for love and marriage and a greenhouse of her own threatened to overwhelm her. Then she took a large drink of cold water and got hold of herself. This wasn't real. He was practicing. He didn't want to marry her. He was using her to perfect his technique. And suddenly she didn't want to be used. She didn't want to play this game anymore. This was not the brainstorming session she'd imagined. That would have been bad enough. But this was worse. His pretending she was one of the women on his list. She should have said no to this dinner back in the office. But it wasn't too late to put a stop to it. She'd call his bluff.

''Yes,'' she said. ''If you put it that way, of course I'd marry you. I can be bought just like anyone else. So you see, you don't need a new plan. The old one will work just fine. All you need to do is to ask the right woman.''

''I thought I just did,'' he muttered.

''See how easy it was?'' she continued breathlessly. ''There's no reason you can't convince any woman to marry you. You just proved it could be done. Can we go home now?''

''Not yet,'' he said. Ben had put the ring in his pocket every time he went out these past weeks. But he'd never gotten far enough to take it out and offer it to someone. Never wanted to. Not until now. He wasn't sure why, didn't know what possessed him, but he reached into his pocket, opened the small velvet-lined box and took out a diamond ring rimmed with rubies that sparkled like a thousand candles.

It wasn't part of the plan, but he reached for Emily's hand and slipped the diamond and ruby ring onto her finger. Her eyes were as wide as the finger bowls on the table. Her face was flushed, and she stared dumbfounded at the huge diamond. Maybe every woman would react that way, but he didn't think so. The others were much too sophisticated, much too jaded to look the way Emily did, as if someone had plucked a star out of the sky and handed it to her.

She was so different from all the women in his life. She was so honest and had so little pretense. He didn't know anyone like her. And so sweet, so affable. Why couldn't he find someone like her to marry him? The truth was, there was no one quite like her. He almost hated to take the ring off her finger. But he had to. He couldn't marry Emily. She was his assistant.

The waiter brought coffee and chocolate mousse as Emily tugged at the ring. She frowned. "I can't…I can't… Can you help me get this ring off?" She held out her hand. He pulled and he yanked, but the ring wouldn't move. It was stuck as if it had been welded onto her finger. As if it had been made for her.

She stood up from the table, tears welling in her large luminous eyes.

"Where are you going?" he asked.

"I'm going to the ladies' room and use some soap on my finger. I—I've got to get this ring off—"

"Stop," he ordered. "Sit down."

She sat down. "What are we going to do?" she asked.

It came to him with a sudden flash of insight. A brilliant idea, the kind that he was famous for in boardrooms across the country. The kind that led to his biggest successes. The solution was crystal-clear. The solution to all his problems.

It was sitting across the table from him. Staring him in the face, out of soft gray eyes behind rimless glasses.

"What are we going to do?" he said. "Isn't it obvious? We're going to get married."

Chapter Two

Ben drove her home, and she noted with relief that the windows of her neighbors' homes were mercifully dark. As far as she knew no curtains rustled, no faces pressed against the glass, no hushed voices said, "Who's that with Emily?" or "What kind of a car is that?" or "Isn't Emily out kind of late?" After living there for four years, she knew many of her neighbors quite well. It wasn't just the garden club. The whole street participated in a potluck every spring and kept watch on vacant houses when neighbors went on vacation.

Presumably no one saw her pull up in an expensive black sports car, no one saw a suave Arab prince leap out to open the door for her and walk her to her front door. They didn't hear her stammer good-night or see her stumble into the house and drop face first onto the sofa as her knees turned to jelly. If they had they would have been on the phone with her the next morning, or maybe even that night, asking questions like "Who was that man you were with?" and

"What kind of a car was that, anyway?" or "Where were you?"

Fortunately no one saw the prince solemnly shake hands with her, and no one heard him calmly tell her he'd see her tomorrow. He didn't say another word about getting married. She told herself it was all a dream. But the ring wasn't. It was real. So real that when she finally got into bed, she couldn't sleep. She tossed and turned, feeling the weight of it on her finger. Feeling the weight of the responsibility of marrying Sheik Ben Ali weigh on her mind. Planning what she'd say when she saw him at the office the next day.

"About last night," she'd say. "I realize you're under a lot of pressure with your thirty-fifth birthday approaching, but you know and I know that I can't marry you, Ben." By that time she'd have somehow worked the ring off her finger so she could carefully place it on his desk. So he could gratefully snatch it back and replace it in its little box where it would stay until he found the right person.

He'd be relieved. Because by now he was no doubt wondering what on earth he'd done—proposing to his assistant—and how he was going to undo it. But she'd make it easy for him to get out of it. That was her job. To make the difficult things in his life easy. To smooth the rough edges. To work behind the scenes so that others could shine. That had always been her job. First in the confines of the large Claybourne family, then out in the world. More than a job, it was her role in life. She was good at it and she was proud of it.

And after she cleared up this little misunderstanding, she would renew her efforts to help him find a wife. Someone suitable. Someone who would understand what he wanted. What he most certainly didn't want was a plain-faced, efficient assistant who was madly in love with him. Who might not be able to hide her feelings for a year. A year!

She wouldn't be able to hide them for a week if she was married to him, sharing the same house or condo or whatever. With a sigh she closed her eyes, buried her face in her pillow and willed herself to go to sleep. She might have fallen asleep if the phone hadn't rung.

"Emily, I've been thinking," he said.

She sat up in bed and clutched the receiver to her ear. "So have I. Listen, Ben, don't worry about a thing. I've thought it through and I…"

"Don't worry? We're getting married in two weeks and you're telling me not to worry? I just got off the phone with my father."

"You didn't…you didn't tell him, did you?"

"Of course I told him. He was delighted, by the way. He says to give you his warmest congratulations."

"He…he remembered me?"

"Vividly." Ben didn't tell her his father had burst into a torrent of excited Arabic, recalling Emily's modest demeanor at the office, her gentle smile and her soft voice, saying she was everything a man could want in a wife. If in fact he was determined to marry an American. Ben didn't have the heart to tell him it was all a sham. That he had no intention of staying married to anyone, especially not prim and proper Emily, for more than a year. He did confess that he wasn't in love with his intended bride, but his father brushed this off like so many grains of sand, repeating once again that love follows marriage and not the reverse.

"But what did you tell him? How did you explain?" she asked.

"Easy. I told him how compatible we were, how easy you are to get along with, how long I've known you. How we complement each other. He was only surprised I hadn't thought of it before. So am I. I just want to tell you how much I appreciate what you're doing for me. And believe me, you'll get your greenhouse, Emily. You'll get a whole arboretum if you want.''

''Thank you,'' she said so faintly that he almost missed it.

''Look, I'm sorry if I woke you, but first thing in the morning I want to announce it to the staff. Then there's the church, the invitations, the reception, your dress, the honeymoon.''

''Honeymoon?'' she gasped.

''Call the travel department and book us a honeymoon somewhere, anywhere, I don't care.'' He realized he was talking faster and louder and that Emily's voice was getting softer and weaker. Perhaps this wasn't the time to be making plans, but time was running out and he'd promised— ''Are you still there?'' he asked.

A long silence. ''Yes, I'm here,'' she said finally.

''Go to bed. Get some sleep. We have a big day ahead of us.''

She didn't answer. The only sound was the click that told him she'd hung up. Ben really didn't have to call her in the middle of the night to outline the schedule for the next day. He called because he was suddenly half-afraid she might have changed her mind. He couldn't really remember if she'd actually said yes at all. But why wouldn't she? It was just a year out of her life. And then she'd have her greenhouse and a large sum of money, and they could get what is called an amicable divorce and go back to working together. Whatever happened, he didn't want to jeopardize their working relationship.

Though Ben had told Emily to go to bed and get some sleep, he was unable to follow his own advice. No anxiety over an important business deal, no corporate concerns ever kept Sheik Ben Ali awake at night. He was blessed by the ability to put all problems out of his mind and get a sound sleep, whether on an airplane, in a desert tent or the most luxurious hotel suite. But tonight, for some mysterious reason, he paced back and forth in front of the picture window in his living room, watching dawn come up over San Francisco Bay before he changed clothes and went to the office.

The first thing Emily did when she arrived that morning was to find a web site on her computer. Then, armed with certain basic questions "to help the bride deal with those seemingly endless choices," she went into Ben's office. She was surprised to see him standing at his window watching the city wake up instead of bent over his desk as usual. When he turned to look at her his eyes were bleary and his tie askew. She had a wild desire to run her hand through his rumpled hair, to feel the thick strands brush against her fingers. She looked away, afraid this crazy desire would show in her eyes. Though her heart thumped so loudly she was afraid he'd hear it, she swallowed hard and took her usual seat facing his desk.

Briskly and competently she asked the questions that the wedding planner suggested under the heading: The Sobering Reality of Planning a Wedding. So sobering, her face felt frozen, as if she'd never smile again. She tried to pretend this was just another workday, this was just another project they were working on together. Only, her icy fingers and her telltale heart told her this was not just another day. This was the beginning of a new era. A frightening new era where the old rules no longer applied.

"Wedding guest list?" she asked.

He rubbed his forehead. "I don't know. Look in my Rolodex under family and invite them all. And your family of course. Yours and mine. And that's it." She nodded, but she couldn't possibly ask her family to a phony wedding and then have to explain later that it was over before it began.

"Ceremony—in a church or not?" she asked.

"Either way. I converted to Christianity in college. My family is Muslim, of course, but they won't expect a traditional ceremony. They're just happy I'm getting married at all."

"Attire—formal or informal?"

"Formal."

"Reception?"

"Doesn't matter."

"Food?"

"I don't care."

"Budget?"

He shrugged.

She stood. She didn't ask about the honeymoon and neither did he. Maybe he would forget about it. Maybe he'd be willing to postpone it. For, say, about twelve months. Then it would be a moot point. "I'll get back to you later," she promised. "As soon as I get some information."

"Good. You know what I said. Let everything else go. The wedding gets top priority. Once we get that over with, we can get on with more important matters."

"Right."

If she didn't understand her boss so well, her feelings might have been hurt by his casual dismissal of this wedding as being a necessary-but-unimportant step in his life. She did understand, but it still hurt deep down. Maybe it was because she knew this was the only wedding she'd ever have. Maybe it was because she knew he was the only man she'd ever love. Whatever it was, she couldn't allow herself the luxury of hurt feelings. She stiffened her spine and lifted her chin and went back to work.

Only later did she remember her plan to give him back

his ring. But she couldn't, even if she'd wanted to, unless she called in someone with a hacksaw to remove it. It was still stuck tightly on her finger. She realized then that she'd come to accept this bizarre wedding as inevitable. She sighed loudly and settled down with her trusty computer and the yellow pages of the phone book, and soothed herself by getting into the swing of problem solving. At least she tried to get into the swing.

But just when she thought she'd have the wedding arrangements settled in no time, the interruptions began. Every time she picked up the phone, someone poked his or her head in the door. If Emily thought she could hide in her office, she was wrong. And if she thought she could keep her plans a secret from even one single person in the company, once the word got out, she was wrong again. The phones rang off the hook until she gave up and let her voice mail kick in. Representatives from every department found some reason to drop by her office. The real reason was to see her ring. She knew that.

So, very patiently she held her left hand out, heard their gasps of surprise at the size and brilliance of the stone, and patiently she accepted their congratulations. And patiently she watched their mouths drop open, knowing it wasn't only the size of the diamond that stunned them, or the rubies or the platinum-and-gold setting, it was disbelief. Disbelief that Sheik Ben Ali was marrying his efficient assistant and not one of the glamorous society women he usually consorted with. She knew what they must be thinking. Why, why, why?

By spending most of the morning on the phone and letting everything else go, since that was what Ben wanted, she was able to accomplish quite a bit by noon, despite the interruptions.

Ben stayed holed up in his office, and she didn't know

what he was doing. Various men in suits came and went. At twelve he called her on the intercom and told her to come into his office. Just to check once again, she tugged at her ring. It was tighter than ever on her finger.

She stepped just inside the door and stood watching him as he plowed through the papers on his desk, signing his name to some and tossing others in the wastebasket. His hair had fallen over his forehead, his tie was loosened and his sleeves were rolled up above the elbows. Was this man really going to marry her, Emily Claybourne, in two weeks? No wonder the whole office was buzzing. No wonder they were asking why.

Why this good-looking, exotically handsome, obscenely rich Arab prince was marrying *her*—a woman who'd never in her life had her nails done, who only went to the beauty salon for an occasional haircut, and bought her clothes off the rack at the discount store. Who had no social sense to speak of and who thought a big evening was one spent at the local garden outlet.

Emily was the only one in the whole office not asking why. She knew why. What she wanted to know was how. How was she going to pull it off? How was she going to pretend to the world that this marriage was for real? And even more important, how was she going to pretend to Ben that she was no more in love with him than he was with her? It was hard enough just working with him, but living with him? She gave a little shiver of fear, and he looked up.

He studied her for a long moment. She hoped he couldn't see beyond the surface. She hoped and prayed he'd never know how she felt about him. She'd have to be especially careful. He was notorious for his sixth sense, which allowed him to get the edge in business deals. He always seemed to know what the other parties were thinking, while keeping his own expression inscrutable. He mustn't ever guess what she was feeling. Never.

Before he had a chance to speak, she opened her notebook computer, sat in the chair across from him and proceeded to give him a report of her morning's activities.

"Good work," he said when she finished. But she had a funny feeling he hadn't been listening to her. He was looking at her in a very strange way.

"Here's what *I've* been doing all morning," he said. "Preparing the contract for you to sign." He held out a sheaf of legal-size papers and pointed to the bottom line.

She reached for the papers in her hand. His hand brushed hers, and she felt her heart leap forward. She tried to read the contract, but her eyes glazed over. Legalese, all of it. All clauses and party-of-the-first-part. She'd never handled contracts. He had lawyers for that. The same lawyers who'd written up these papers for her to sign. She took a pen from her suit pocket to sign her name on the dotted line.

"Wait a minute," he said, grabbing the papers out of her hand as the pen made a long scrawl into the margin. "Aren't you going to read it first?"

"I'm sure it's fine."

"How are you sure? I might be going to cheat you."

"Are you?" she asked.

"No, of course not. I think I've been more than fair. So do my lawyers."

"Then why the contract?" she asked.

"Come on, Emily. Don't be naive. I can't take any chances. And neither should you. By signing these papers, you accept my offer and you promise to stay married to me for one year, to assume the life of a married woman and all that entails."

"All that entails," she repeated. She took a deep breath. She was afraid to ask what it meant, but she had to. "What does that mean exactly?'' Cooking? Cleaning? Socializing? Sex? Her face reddened at the thought. At the word she couldn't say.

"What do you think it means?" There was a glimmer in his eyes that made her face turn the color of a Crimson Glory rose. Could he be teasing her? No, it wasn't possible. It had always been strictly business between them. The next time she looked the glimmer was gone. It was back to business.

"I...I don't know what it means," she stammered. "I suppose it means socializing or something."

"Or something," he repeated. "It doesn't mean sex if that's what you're worried about."

She managed to shrug her shoulders as if it had never occurred to her to be worried about sex. Truthfully she was terrified at the idea of sex with Ben. She could only imagine the humiliation of a virgin making love with an experienced Lothario. So she was relieved to have the matter out in the open. And to find she had nothing to worry about. He didn't want to engage in any sexual activity with her any more than she did with him. This was not that kind of marriage. Thank heavens.

She picked up her pen and reached for the papers.

"Don't you want to know what you get in return?"

"You already told me. A greenhouse."

"Much more than a greenhouse. A considerable sum of money."

"Thank you." She stood up, leaned over his desk and scribbled her name on the dotted line.

"Don't thank *me*. You're doing me a huge favor. I haven't forgotten that."

"I do have a question."

He smiled. "Just one?"

"Will I...I mean I assume I'll continue working."

"Of course. I couldn't get along without you."

"Thank you. But you said something about 'a woman's place...'"

"Is in the home. Yes, but I didn't mean you."

She pressed her lips together to keep them from trembling. Of course he didn't mean her. He meant his *real* wife, when and if he had one, who'd be at home waiting for him in his penthouse condominium when he got home from work, with a fire burning in the Swedish fireplace in his book-lined den, a delicious dinner simmering on the restaurant-style stove in the tiled kitchen. Never mind that he said he didn't want a real wife. Men always said that until they met the right woman. Then they changed their minds fast enough.

"Now," he said, rubbing his hands together. "Take the afternoon off. Get your hair done and buy a new dress. We have to have dinner with the chairman of the board of Remsen Oil."

"We?" She couldn't help it, her voice squeaked in surprise. Would she ever get used to being part of a "we"?

"Yes, I was going by myself, but now that I have a fiancée..."

She sighed. "You have to take me." He didn't want to take her, but if it fit into the program...

"Yes. He's bringing his wife, I'm bringing my fiancée. I'll pick you up at seven."

She nodded and turned to leave the office, her feet feeling like lead. Dinner with the chairman of the board of a huge oil company and his wife? This wasn't her idea of a good time. She'd always felt sorry for Ben going off to a business dinner while she got to go home, take off her stockings, put on her coveralls and sink her hands into the dirt in her garden. When she signed that contract, she didn't know it would mean buying new clothes and having her hair done and giving up her precious free time. But she should have. Any other woman would have known, but not her. She ran her fingers over the neat knot she'd twisted her hair into that morning and glanced down at her plain navy suit. Of course, no wonder he suggested changes in her appearance. She looked like an efficient assistant and not anybody's fiancée, especially not Sheik Ben Ali's fiancée.

"Wait a minute," he called as she was about to close the door behind her. "I don't remember where you live."

Patiently she turned back, wrote her address on a memo pad and handed it to him. Then, without another word she left the office early for the first time in three years.

Ben sat at his desk, absently rapping his pencil against his coffee mug for a long time after Emily had left his office. She'd signed the contract. It was too late for either one of them to back out of it. But he couldn't help but wonder how he'd gotten into this mess. Yes, he needed a wife. Yes, Emily was smart and capable, but while she knew everything about him, he knew nothing about her life outside of the office.

She might have a live-in boyfriend. Or a kennel full of greyhounds. Maybe she grew mushrooms in her basement, or lived with twenty-five cats like certain spinsters one read about. Maybe she intended to bring them with her to his penthouse. The boyfriend, the hounds, the mushrooms and the cats. He didn't even know if she preferred to live in a house or an apartment or a commune, or if she had a mother and a father.

He didn't know what he expected from this marriage, but he knew what she didn't expect. Sex. The immense relief on her face when he told her that wasn't part of the deal startled him. Was the thought of sex with him so distasteful? Apparently so. Of course it wasn't part of the deal.

That would complicate matters in the extreme. But still, her obvious distaste had bruised his ego.

By the time Emily staggered to her stucco cottage from the bus stop in the decidedly unfashionable Sunset section of the city, she'd begun her modest transformation. But her efforts had taken their toll. She dragged her feet past row houses that had been built during a postwar building boom on what was once sand dunes. Her arms ached from hauling the shopping bags around town, looking for the right shoes for the right dress. Peggy Grant, her neighbor and fellow rose grower, set her pruning shears down and called to her from over the fence.

"Whoooeee," she said, planting her hands on her ample hips. "New hairdo. Don't you look smart?"

Emily dropped the boxes and bags at the front door and went to the fence that separated the two small yards. She raked her hand self-consciously through her new short curls. "You don't think it's too extreme?"

"Extremely pretty, that's what I think. What's up? Got a big date?" Peggy asked with a wink.

"No, no, just a business dinner with my boss. But I thought I needed a new look." *He* thought she needed a new look was more like it. *He* thought she didn't look good enough the way she was. He was right of course. But that didn't make it any easier to put herself in the hands of a hairdresser and buy a new dress. She'd never spent so much money at one time in her life. And even then she didn't know what he'd say when he saw her in her new dress. Probably something like "Emily, what's gotten into you?" or "What have you done to yourself?" or "Who do you think you're fooling?" Because even with her new hairdo and dress she was still her same old self. And she still looked nothing like any woman he'd ever dated. Nor did she want to.

"Your boss, the sheik?" Peggy asked, her mouth opened wide in surprise. "You have a date with your boss?"

"It's not really a date," Emily said, plucking a faded rose from a trailing vine. "It's more of a business dinner."

"Oh." Peggy's face fell. "Well still... Want me to come over and do your makeup?"

"Makeup? I don't normally wear makeup."

"You don't normally go out with your boss, either."

"That's right." Emily surveyed the round, kindly face of her neighbor and wondered if she should tell her now or wait until later. Since Peggy and the other garden club members would be the only ones she'd invite to the wedding, maybe she ought to tell her now. She rehearsed several ways of breaking the news:

By the way, I'm not just going out with my boss, I'm going to marry him.

Speaking of my boss, we're getting married.

If you're not doing anything June 23, Peggy, I'd like you to come to my wedding.

If you have time next week, I wonder if you'd help me pick out a wedding dress, because, you see...

No, none of those would do.

"Peggy," she said. "I'd love it if you'd do my makeup. And by the way...by the way..."

"Yes?"

"I have something to tell you."

"What is it? For heaven's sake, Emily, what's wrong? You look like you just lost your best friend."

Emily gave a mirthless chuckle. "Really? That's funny because I have some good news, really good news. I—I'm getting married."

Peggy's eyes widened behind her bifocals until they were the size of cabbage roses. "You're what?"

"I know. I'm just as surprised as you are."

"But I didn't even know you were dating anyone."

"Neither did I," Emily confessed.

"Who is the lucky man?" Peggy asked.

"You've heard me speak of my boss—"

"The richest, most eligible bachelor in the whole city, maybe the whole world. A bona fide Arab sheik?"

"Uh…yes, that's the one."

"You're not going to tell me you're getting married to an Arab prince, are you?"

Emily bit her lip and nodded. "But it's not what you think."

"Is it what *you* think?" Her friend asked, her round eyes soft and sympathetic.

"More or less," Emily said, hoping she could avoid any more questions about her strange and unusual marriage. "I'd better go in and get dressed."

Bless her heart, Peggy didn't ask another question. She only said, "I'll be over with my makeup kit, in what…a half hour?"

"Okay. Fine. Thanks." What else could she say without hurting Peggy's feelings? She could say *I don't want to look like I'm trying to impress anyone, especially not Ben. He's seen me without makeup for three years. He asked me to marry him without makeup, so nothing I do now will change anything.* Of course there was the chairman of the board of Remsen. Maybe she ought to wear makeup to impress him and his wife.

At seven o'clock she stood in the middle of her small living room wearing a sleeveless, black crepe dress, pearl earrings and choker, courtesy of her next-door neighbor, and skillfully applied foundation and a hint of blush also courtesy of Peggy's skillful fingers. The look of approval on Peggy's face as she backed out the door a half hour ago told Emily she looked different. Very different. In a good way. Of course that was partly because she'd taken off her glasses and put them in her small black purse.

When Ben's car pulled up in front of the house, she shivered with apprehension and wondered if she looked *too* different. He himself looked just as he always did, suave, perfectly groomed, perfectly tailored in a dark business suit. When she opened the door, he stood there staring at her for a long, endless moment. Then she knew for sure, she *did* look too different.

"Would you like to come in?" she asked. "Or..."

For once he didn't finish her sentence. He didn't say a word. He just continued to stand there and stare with those dark smoldering eyes, letting his gaze travel from the tips of her shoes to the top of her short brown curls. She had no idea what he thought. Probably that she'd overdone it. After all, it was just a business dinner.

They might have stood there in silence for an hour, Emily teetering back and forth in her new high-heeled sandals, Ben with one hand on the door frame, the other in his pocket, if Ben's cell phone hadn't rung. As if roused from a deep stupor, he grabbed it from his pocket.

"Yes, Tom?... You do? Oh, I'm sorry to hear that... Of course you should... Of course I can... I will... I certainly will. Take care of yourself."

Ben stuffed the phone into the vest pocket of his jacket and finally walked through the doorway of his fiancée's house. His fiancée. How strange to have a fiancée after all these years. Especially a fiancée who'd transformed herself in the space of one afternoon into a stranger. Gone was his reliable, trustworthy, plain and efficient administrative assistant, Emily Claybourne, and in her place there was a stranger.

"Emily?" he said, unable to keep from staring at this creature in the black dress. Unable to reconcile the vision of a stylish young woman in pearls with the plain assistant he relied on for her unwavering support and sense of duty. What happened? What had she done? He'd expected a new dress, but didn't this dress show a little too much of her smooth skin, wasn't it a little too tight, cut a little low in front? He'd expected a touch of lipstick maybe, in honor of the chairman of the board they were dining with, but she'd transformed herself, and he wasn't sure he liked the transformation.

He liked and respected the old Emily he'd known for three years. He hoped she'd be back on Monday morning, because the woman standing in front of him in the form-fitting dress, showing way too much of her curves and her long legs, stirred unwelcome feelings and made him downright uneasy.

"Who was that on the phone?" she asked.

"That was Tom Spandler. He canceled. He's sick. The dinner's off."

She nodded, took a step backward and then she fell rather than sat down in a large armchair and knotted her fingers in her lap. Her relief was palpable and matched his own. Off the hook. She didn't say it, but that's how she felt. He did, too.

"I'm sorry. You've gone to a lot of trouble. Got yourself all dressed up. For nothing." All dressed up? She'd undergone some magical transformation and now had nowhere to go. "But that doesn't mean we can't go, anyway," he added politely.

"But we don't have to, do we?"

"Of course not, I just thought you'd want to. You're a strange girl, you know."

"I know."

"Any other woman would insist on dinner after she'd gone to all the trouble of dressing up for it. But not you. If we don't go out, what will you do for dinner?"

"I don't know. Make an omelet, I guess."

"In that dress?"

She smiled at the picture of herself cracking eggs in her new dress. "I'll change into my jeans and sweatshirt first."

"What kind?"

"Long-sleeved, fleece-lined. With the name of my school on the front."

"I mean what kind of omelet."

"Oh. I don't know. Mushrooms, maybe, with cheese. Whatever I've got in the fridge."

"Sounds good," he said, unaware that a wistful note had crept into his deep voice. How long had it been since he'd eaten a home-cooked meal? His father told him to hire a cook, but he'd never wanted one. He was never there at mealtime, and a cook would always be asking when he'd be home and what he wanted for dinner. Almost as bad as a wife. No, his system of lunch-on-the-run and business dinners was the best.

She gave him a quick, curious glance. "Would you— you're welcome to stay for dinner, if you'd like."

He could tell by the tone of her voice she was only being polite. She was just as glad as he that the dinner was canceled. "Oh, I couldn't impose on you. Not at the last minute like this. You've probably got things to do."

"I've got to take this dress off, that's what I've got to do," she said, standing up. "And the necklace." She reached behind her neck and fumbled with the clasp. He watched the smooth fabric of the dress stretch across her breasts, and he drew in a sharp breath. Did she have to take the necklace off here in front of him? Of course he could leave. He'd already told her he couldn't impose. But he didn't leave.

Instead he stepped behind her and grabbed the clasp out of her hands so that he could do it himself. In the process he got a whiff of some subtle perfume. Emily...wearing perfume? He'd never known her to wear perfume before. If she had, he would have known it, working so closely with her all these years. Tendrils of short curls brushed the back of her neck. She'd never worn her hair so short, had she? Never had curls of any kind. Had her skin always been that smooth? Her neck that slender? After an eternity he was finally able to snap the clasp open and remove the pearls.

"Thank you," she said in a breathless voice as he dropped them into her open palm. "I'll just be a minute." Then she went down the hall and into what he supposed was her bedroom.

That's when he could have left. Should have left. Should have shouted goodbye at her through her bedroom door. She didn't want him there. He didn't want to be there. Her invitation was halfhearted at best. He was imposing and taking advantage of her good nature. If he hadn't said "Sounds good," he'd be halfway home by now. But he did say it, and she did invite him, and it would be rude of him to leave now. Without making an excuse.

He took his jacket off, then his tie, and rolled up his sleeves. Now was his chance to look around for the clues to Emily's identity. So far it didn't look like she had a live-in boyfriend or a kennel in the backyard, but he couldn't be sure.

The only thing he was sure of was there was well-worn comfortable furniture in her living room. A large sofa slip-covered in some off-white nubby fabric against the wall. A deep armchair in the corner with a hassock in front of it with a reading lamp where he imagined she spent many hours curled up with a book. A giant fern hung from the ceiling and there were roses everywhere filling the air with their fragrance. A huge vase of pale pink flowers on the mantel, a small snifter with one yellow rose on the coffee table and a large bouquet of deep red roses on the windowsill.

Through the open window he saw roses climbing the fence between her house and the one next door. He realized that Emily had kept his office filled with these same roses and he never knew she grew them herself. Face it, he never knew anything about her at all. He still didn't.

From behind the fence a straw hat popped up and under it a woman's round face. She raised her eyebrows when she saw him in the window, then she smiled and waved.

He waved back.

He was about to examine a framed photograph on the wall when the doorbell rang and he answered it. Two small girls in brown uniforms stood on the front step.

"Hello, mister," said the one with braids. "Would your wife like to buy some Girl Scout cookies?"

Chapter Three

Ben had a warm spot in his heart for kids. His brother told him he should never have any of his own or he'd spoil them rotten, the way he did his nieces and nephews. It was probably a good thing he was never getting married for real and thus never having any children of his own.

"*I'd* be glad to buy some cookies," he said, not bothering to mention he didn't have a wife—not yet. "I'll take all you've got."

The girls looked at each other in surprise and giggled loudly.

"We've got 'bout two hundred boxes in the van." The girl with the gap between her front teeth gestured to the van at the curb with its engine idling.

"Is that all?" he asked and they giggled again.

After writing a check to the Girl Scouts, he unloaded the van, stacked the boxes of cookies inside the front door, received profuse thanks from the child's mother who said the girls would surely win a prize for the most sales on the first day of the cookie sale.

He came back to find Emily standing in the middle of her living room with her hands on her hips staring at the mountain of cookies. He was relieved to see she was dressed in baggy jeans and her shapeless, fleece-lined sweatshirt. That way he was able to concentrate on other things besides the shape of her body. She looked more relaxed, the worry lines gone from her forehead. She was once again wearing her rimless glasses, and her face was washed clean of makeup. Only her hairstyle was different. Ever since he'd known her she'd worn long hair pulled back behind her ears, but now short curls framed her small face giving her a decidedly pixie look. A very puzzled pixie.

"What on earth..." she said.

"I hope you like cookies," he said.

"I love cookies, especially the thin mints, but I can't eat all these. A box or two would have done fine. What possessed you?"

"Those little girls. They were wearing uniforms and I couldn't resist. Also I like to encourage free enterprise and salesmanship. If I had a child, I'd see to it—" He broke off abruptly. "Besides, I like cookies, too."

Emily nodded. She wondered, with his attitude toward marriage, if he wanted children. She knew he doted on his nieces and nephews, sent presents to them on the slightest pretext, but had never heard him say he wanted children of his own.

"I'll never eat them all," she said. "You'll have to take half of them home."

"Or we could take them to the office," he said.

There it was, that "we" again. Emily didn't know if she'd ever get used to it. She'd been on her own for four years, now, and it was going to take some time to get used to being part of a "we." More than a year, so why bother?

"Well, sit down and relax and I'll fix us something to eat." What she meant was, Sit down here in the living room and I'll go into the kitchen by myself and fix us something to eat. But Ben followed her into the kitchen and straddled a kitchen chair as if it were the most natural thing for an Arab sheik to watch his assistant crack eggs into a bowl.

"I owe you one for this," he said.

"For making you an omelet? No, you don't," she assured him. She certainly didn't want to continue this tit-for-tat arrangement or she'd never have a minute to herself. It was bad enough having to endure the proximity of her sexy boss at work, but now he'd invaded her space at home, too, forcing her to be constantly on her guard. It was exhausting. It was enervating. She felt better now that she'd changed into her old clothes, but not normal. She wouldn't feel normal until he'd left her house and gone home. She wondered, for the one hundredth time, how she was ever going to marry this man. "You just took me to dinner last night," she reminded him.

He ran his hand through his hair until it was so rumpled it made him look boyish and approachable and more like the man next door than an oil-rich sheik. Provided the man next door was breathtakingly handsome. "Was it just last night? It seems like eons ago."

She nodded in agreement as she rummaged in her refrigerator for the ingredients.

"Do you like to cook?" he asked.

"Yes." But not when you're sitting there watching me.

"Because I thought I'd either hire a cook, once we get married, or we'd just order out every night."

An egg slipped out of her hand and fell on the floor. That's what happens when your palms are damp. When you're on the edge of cracking up yourself, she thought. Did he have to choose this moment to talk about getting married? Just for a few minutes she was trying to forget. But he had to bring it up. As if she wasn't nervous enough having him in her kitchen. She'd had many dreams about Ben, but not one of them featured her making dinner for him. She couldn't help but think that deep down he still believed a woman's place was in the home. So now that he saw her in her home, what did he think?

He grabbed a paper towel and cleaned up the mess for her, and she took another egg from the refrigerator. Then there was a knock on the back door. She sighed loudly and opened the door just a crack. It was Peggy.

"I thought you were going out," she said with a swift, inquisitive glance at Emily's sweatshirt.

"There was a change of plans," Emily said, hoping she'd take the hint and leave. Hoping she wouldn't come in and see Ben and say something that would embarrass them both.

"I see," Peggy said. "I was wondering if I could borrow— Oh, I didn't know you had company. I'll come back later."

Emily wiped her hands on her apron. "No, it's okay. Come on in."

Peggy slipped into the kitchen and fixed her gaze on Ben, who got to his feet as Emily introduced him.

"Peggy, this is Ben Ali Mansour, my…my boss."

"Pleased to met you." Peggy beamed at Ben, and he charmed her by asking about her garden. Emily had seen him dazzle new acquaintances at least one hundred times, but only in a business situation. He'd somehow find out the person's interests and then get them to talk about them. Everyone loves talking about themselves, and Ben was the ultimate good listener. While Emily chopped and grated and sautéed, Ben drew Peggy out until Peggy finally excused herself and left without whatever it was she was going to borrow.

Emily had never wished for a dining room or a dining room table until now. Now the simple pine kitchen table seemed impossibly small for two people, especially if those two people had been thrown together by fate and didn't belong together at all. She threw a homespun cloth over the table and set two mismatched plates filled with fluffy omelets and toast. When she finally sat down, her knees bumped into his. Her gaze clashed with his until she fastened her eyes on her plate. They ate in awkward silence. Sure, they'd sometimes eaten sandwiches from a local deli in his office while in the middle of a project, but this was altogether different. It was too intimate, too awkward to have him here in her modest kitchen, but it didn't seem to bother Ben at all. He was too busy eating. He acted like he hadn't eaten in weeks, and when he finished he said it was the best omelet he'd ever had.

"How about some cookies for dessert?" he asked.

What could she say? Please take those cookies and go home? This was all happening too fast. She wanted to get rid of him. She didn't want him hanging around her humble house any longer. She didn't know how to act in front of him. At the office they had fallen into a comfortable routine over the years. But now everything was different. She was hit by a wave of sadness when she realized they could never go back to being the way they were.

She had a sinking feeling that she'd never again be comfortable around him. She was once happy in her role as his employee. She'd come to accept the fact that she was in love with a man who'd never love her back. In a way it was a safe situation. As long as he didn't know. But when he'd stepped over the threshold of her front door tonight, he'd changed the equation forever. It was all his fault for asking her to marry him. It was her fault, too. Her fault for falling in love with him. And her fault for agreeing to this crazy scheme.

"No, thanks, Ben. Why don't you take them home with you?"

"I'll do that." He thanked her for the dinner, and she followed him to the living room. But before he picked up one single box of cookies, he paused in front of the picture she had framed on the wall. He shot her an inquisitive look.

"My family," she volunteered. Oh, no, why hadn't she removed that picture from the wall? Now he'd know she had a family. She couldn't pretend to be an orphan, and he would wonder why her family wasn't coming to the wedding.

"You've never said anything about your family," he remarked.

"You never asked."

He nodded and then turned back to the photograph of the Claybourne clan taken a few years ago. "Where are you?" he asked.

"There I am, in the back row."

"Are you sure? I can't see your face."

"That's because I'm short. But take my word for it, it's me."

"Who's this handsome couple in the front row?"

"My parents."

She half expected him to say, But you don't look a thing like your mother with her flowing dark hair and her statuesque body...or your father with his mane of gray hair and his wide smile...or any of your attractive brothers and sisters. But he didn't. Of course not. He was far too polite. But he must have thought it. Everyone did.

"Who are the others?"

She pointed as she named them. "My sister Robin, my sister Helen, my brother Paul, my other brother Jared."

"They're all so tall, so good-looking."

"Except for me," she said matter-of-factly. "I'm the oldest child and the shortest and the plainest. That's funny, isn't it?" She gave him a little smile to show him how funny it was, but deep down it still hurt to have him see the startling contrast between her and the rest of her family. Ben tilted his head to one side and studied her face.

She knew he couldn't deny it. He didn't even try. She was the ugly duckling in a family of beauties. Not only that but she was the only one with absolutely no talent. She knew it. She thought she'd long ago come to terms with it. But there were times when she longed to be beautiful, too, and to be the center of attention. But it wasn't going to happen.

"What do they do?" he asked.

"They're all actors or singers or artists of one kind or another. Struggling to make a go of it. In between jobs they wait tables or sell encyclopedias door-to-door."

"Where do you fit in?" he asked.

"Me? I'm the sensible one. The serious one. The one with no talent. The one who took care of the details like paying the bills and buying the groceries, keeping track of their schedules."

"They must be lost without you."

"Oh, no. Not at all. They thought they would be, but they manage just fine. No one's indispensable, you know."

He raised his eyebrows. "I'm not sure about that."

"It's true."

"Didn't you ever want to be in the front row yourself or take center stage?" he asked.

"No, of course not," she assured him. "Besides, I told you, I'm not talented."

"Not talented? You can read a spread sheet upside down. You are a master of details, and you're a whiz at long-term corporate strategy."

She shrugged off these compliments. "That's different. Actually, I'm lucky, in a way. Lucky that I had no talent or illusions about myself. I went to college and majored in business. You can imagine what they thought of that. Bo-o-o-ring!" She smiled because she knew that deep down they were proud of her. As for her, she admired them immensely. Sure there'd been occasional pangs of jealousy, and maybe she would never conquer those feelings completely, but things were better since she'd moved away and made a life for herself outside their magnetic field.

It made her feel good to know her family respected and understood her. But they wouldn't understand her marrying someone who didn't love her. She knew what they'd say. "Hold out, Emily. This is not the right man for you. He's a sheik, for heaven's sake. You're not the type to marry a sheik." As if she didn't know.

He examined the photo again. "Well, I'm looking forward to meeting them all at the wedding," he said.

"They won't be there. They're all pretty busy with jobs or summer stock or voice lessons or something."

"Too busy to come to your wedding?"

"It's not a real wedding. I mean, I wouldn't want them to think...I wouldn't want them to be disappointed when we call it quits, so I don't intend to tell them about it. What they don't know won't hurt them." What she meant was she wouldn't want her family to be hurt and disappointed for her sake. And they would be, unless she told them in advance the strange circumstances of her getting married. They'd never understand a marriage of convenience. They were great believers in romantic love. She could just hear them now. "Convenient for who?" They were all too dreamy and romantic and impractical. They were always asking if she'd met anyone "special." "It's different for you," she said.

"Not that different. My family will be just as disappointed when we get a divorce. Maybe more so. After all, you're still young, with many chances to remarry, but I'm almost thirty-five. While divorce is unusual in my country, here in the U.S. it's more common and not such a tragedy, especially if there are no children involved. But the divorce is a year away, so why worry about it now?" he asked.

She nodded, but she *was* worried about it. She was worried about the wedding, she was worried about the marriage and she was worried about the divorce, too. But she was most worried about hiding her true feelings. It was hardest when he stood next to her, so close her shoulder brushed his arm, so close she could smell the faint scent of sandalwood soap on his skin. She told herself it was just because her house was so small. So small he filled every room with his presence.

Things would be better when they lived in his penthouse apartment with its ten-foot-high rooms, where she could take refuge in the library or the roof-top patio or her room. Surely, she would have her own room to which she could escape.

She yawned and stared pointedly at the door, but he didn't seem to take the hint. Dinner was over, it was time to go. Instead he lifted a vase of roses and inhaled deeply.

"Do you grow these yourself?"

"Yes, it's my hobby."

"They're beautiful. Aren't they hard to grow?"

"Well..." She drew her eyebrows together. Was he really that interested in roses or was he trying to postpone his departure for some reason? Or draw her out the way he'd done to her neighbor? It was almost as if he didn't want to go home.

"That depends," she said thoughtfully. "You have to follow the rules, of course. Plant in the spring. Choose a protected spot away from the wind, open to sunlight at least several hours a day. A deep rich loam is best, thought hybrids do well in sandy soil, which is what I've got here." She glanced at his face. His eyes had a faraway look in them. "I'm afraid I've told you more than you want to know about roses. But it's your fault. You asked."

He nodded. And she continued. She knew she ought to shoo him out the door, but for some reason she wanted to keep talking.

"Of course, when I get my greenhouse, I'll be able to grow new varieties from seedlings. This one is called Good News," she said pointing to a pale pink flower. "And this one is the Rubiayat. If you like, you could take a few home with you."

"No, I couldn't. They belong here. They even smell like you." He paused. "All right, I'll take just one."

She pulled a magnificent Peace rose from the vase, yellow with pink shadings at the edges of the petals, and pricked her finger with a thorn. "Oooh."

"What happened? You've hurt yourself."

She put the rose on the table and held up her finger to show him it was nothing. Nothing but a drop of blood on the skin. But instead of being relieved, he looked alarmed. He took her hand in his, pressed his lips to her finger and held it there. His eyes were dark and warm with sympathy. She tried to tell him not to worry. She'd pricked herself a hundred times or more, but she couldn't speak. There was a lump in her throat and her mouth was dry. His lips burned her skin. She warned herself not to get excited. It meant nothing. But it was the most erotic thing that ever happened to her. A small burning knot of desire started somewhere deep inside her and threatened to burst into flames.

She swallowed hard and tried to pull her finger away. But she didn't try hard enough. All her senses were focused on her finger and on the sweet pressure of his lips. All she could think of was how it would feel if his lips met hers and he kissed her. The thought made her feel dizzy and lightheaded. The room spun around and her knees threatened to collapse.

Ben caught her just before she lost her balance. With his arm tightly around her waist he held her against his chest.

"Emily, what's wrong? Is it the sight of blood? Is that it?"

For just one moment she rested her head against his shoulder and let him hold her. Instead of being the supporter, she let herself be supported for a change. Just for a minute. Then she took a deep breath and pulled back.

"No, no, I'm fine," she insisted breathlessly. She felt the room slowly stop spinning and come to a halt.

"Are you sure?" he asked. "You look so pale."

"Of course I'm sure," she said. "Now let's get the cookies into your car."

But he wouldn't let her help him load his car. He insisted she sit on her sofa. She felt ridiculous acting like an invalid because she'd pricked her finger. But it was better than acting like a lovesick loon. Yes, let him think she was the type that fainted at the sight of her own blood. It was better than the truth. That she'd almost fainted at the thought of him kissing her. What would happen if he actually did it? She pushed the thought from her mind. It wasn't going to happen.

Ben left the cookies in his car. He would take them to the office the next day and distribute them there. He rode up in the elevator to the twenty-second floor of his building with the Peace rose in his hand. Once in his apartment he stuck it in a glass of water in his book-lined den. The fragrance seemed to follow him everywhere he went. From his bedroom to the kitchen and back again. Like the memory of Emily's soft skin, it haunted him.

He opened his briefcase and emptied the papers onto the dining room table. He had work to do, but he couldn't seem to concentrate. He remembered thinking he'd learn something about his future wife by seeing where she lived. But he'd learned more than he'd bargained for. He'd learned that Emily saw herself as a supporting player at home with her family and with him at work. He'd learned that she had no idea how talented she was in her own way. And no idea how striking she looked in that black cocktail dress. So striking he was relieved when she took it off. She was a superb cook and a wonderful gardener. He didn't think he needed either a cook or a gardener. But as long as they came with the wife…who was he to complain?

And she was going to be his wife. For a year. Only a year. Then he'd go back to his old life, back to the social scene, the parties and receptions and always a different woman on his arm. A woman who knew the score. Who knew how beautiful she was and would never take a back seat to anyone. A woman he wouldn't have to convince she had talent and looks. A woman who was looking for a good time and that was all. Not for the first time that evening he wondered if he shouldn't have looked a little harder, a little longer for a wife like that. Because being married to Emily was not going to be as simple as he'd thought.

Emily was much more serious than the type of woman he'd had in mind. Much more modest and unassuming than any woman he'd ever dated. She could never compete with any of those women. Not that she wanted to. Not that he wanted her to. He just hoped the transition would be smooth—from administrative assistant to wife and back again. He knew if anyone could do it, she could.

As he lay in his king-size bed that night he could smell that single rose all the way from his den. It reminded him of Emily, of her shy smile and her soft gray eyes and her long legs. He wondered what she would have done if he'd given in to his impulses and kissed the back of her neck when he took her necklace off. He tried to imagine her response.

Would she have jumped, screamed or slapped him? Or would she have turned around and put her arms around his neck and kissed him on the mouth? Not very likely. Though she *had* leaned against him there in her living room and put her head on his shoulder. And then he'd had a crazy urge to wrap his arms around her and tell her everything would be all right.

He rubbed his chin with the back of his hand as a smile stole across his face. She was clearly uneasy having him in her house, invading her space. He knew she wanted him to leave, but he had a hard time tearing himself away. He liked seeing her eyes light up when she talked about her roses, liked hearing her talk about her family, and he wished he could meet them, to see her interact with them. She had no idea how her smile transformed her plain face, how her cheeks turned as pink as a rose when she was excited about something. He'd found himself looking for excuses to stay longer.

As the hours ticked by, he was on his way to another sleepless night and all because of Emily. Finally he got up and put the rose in the refrigerator where he couldn't smell it any longer. Then and only then was he able to go to sleep.

* * *

For Emily the next two weeks sped by in a flurry of prenuptial activities. She was so busy she couldn't think—which was precisely what she wanted. Because if she stopped to think, she might have jumped on a plane for somewhere, anywhere and not come back. But running away from her problems was not her way. Not good old reliable Emily, the sane, sensible one.

Emily was the one who held everything together. At home or at the office. She wasn't going to change now, on the eve of her wedding. She discovered one way to keep her sanity was to pretend that she was planning someone else's wedding. As long as she kept herself aloof emotionally from the preparations, she was fine.

But shopping for a wedding dress brought an abrupt halt to her game of pretend. Armed with Ben's credit card, and his order to spare no expense, she took Peggy with her to the bridal salon of the biggest and best department store in the city. While the saleswoman brought in dress after dress and she tried them on, she could no longer distance herself from the wedding. That was her in that three-way mirror. She was going to be a bride. She, Emily Claybourne, was going to marry Sheik Ben Ali. She was going to be the bride, the center of attention. The reality hit her in the middle of her chest like the bouquet of lilies her sister had deliberately thrown at her at her wedding last year.

That was her in that empire-waist, ivory satin with lace detailing. That pale, nervous-looking woman. That was also her in the taffeta column dress with the train. And the silk tulle and satin ribbon gown with the antique lace veil. After what seemed like hours of agony, modeling dresses in front of the mirror, she finally settled on a famous designer lace-bodice gown with organza skirt and a beaded chapel train. By that time she was so numb she didn't know a Vera

Wang from an Isaac Mizrahi. She no longer knew if she wanted satin or silk or lace. Or what was the most becoming. But the saleswoman knew. As she slid the dress over Emily's head and it settled on her shoulders and clung to her curves, both the saleswoman and Peggy gasped.

"It's perfect."

"Beautiful."

At that point Emily would have said yes to anything. She still had a list of things to do that day, but they wouldn't let her go yet. She had to have shoes and jewelry to go with the dress. She said yes to the shoes but no to the jewelry. Then she left the dress with the alterations department and rushed off in Ben's chauffeured car he insisted she use.

The best part of these prenuptial activities was that she rarely saw Ben. She didn't have time. She would give him a report once a day and then she was off. He usually barely looked up from his work, as if he was too busy to think about something so unimportant as his wedding. He might also have been having second thoughts about this whole fiasco, she thought. She certainly was.

The day she bought the dress she stopped by the office on her way to the caterer, but Ben wasn't there. Instead, seated in his swivel chair and twirling a pencil between his fingers was his father, resplendent in his native dress, a white robe and a kerchief over his head with a thick gold cord twisted to hold it in place.

"Come in, my dear," he said with a courtly bow. "I want to speak to you."

Chapter Four

Emily gasped in surprise. Though the wedding was only days away she didn't expect to see any of his family already. In fact, she only expected to see them on her wedding day. That was one good thing about the honeymoon, they would leave for the San Juan Islands after the reception with no time for embarrassing questions from his family. Such as, "When will you have children?" "Are you going to quit your job?" or "Where's your family, Emily?"

But it was too late to back out of the office and pretend she hadn't seen the old sheik. He was on his feet in a flash and was kissing her on both cheeks before she could even say hello.

"My dear Emily," he said, holding her by the shoulders so he could take a long look at her. "You look like a bride already, so radiant and more beautiful than ever. My son is very lucky."

"Oh, no," she protested, feeling a blush creep up her cheeks. "I'm the lucky one."

He insisted she sit down, and he picked up Ben's phone and ordered tea and brushed aside Emily's protests that she couldn't stay.

"You're here to see Ben, of course, but as you see he isn't here. I've ordered him to take the day off, and I'm sitting in for him."

Emily stifled a smile, wondering when the last time was that anyone had ordered Ben to do anything at all.

"Truth to tell," said the sheik, as the man from the lunchroom brought in two cups of tea and set the tray on Ben's desk. "I'm very happy to have a moment alone with you."

"Thank you," she murmured accepting the cup he held out and wondering what he wanted with her. Wondering if Ben would look just like him someday, still trim at age sixty, with lines in his face that only added to his character. They had the same dark brown eyes and thick dark hair.

"Marriage is a big commitment. Both in your country and mine. But there are differences. In my country marriage is forever. We have very few divorces." he said. "Do you know why?"

"I-is it because of pressure from the family?" she asked.

"Partly. But it is mostly because we favor arranged marriages. We don't believe in those illusions of romance and self-fulfillment so popular in this country. We believe that marriage is a union of two families."

"But what about love?"

"Love, yes, I'm glad you asked that," he said, setting his cup on the tray. "Love comes with time. Love comes when one has chosen a suitable mate, or better yet, parents who are wiser and more experienced in the ways of the world have chosen."

Her heart fell. "I suppose you would have chosen someone else for Ben," she said.

"I did choose someone else for him, the daughter of my best friend. But he, being headstrong and schooled in America, did not follow my advice. He only told me he was not worthy of the young woman. I must say I was disappointed."

"I'm sorry," Emily murmured, her eyes on her teacup.

"Don't be sorry," Ben's father said emphatically. "It was years ago, and that is not why I am telling you this. I am telling you because I am happy that you are to be his bride. Long ago I resigned myself to his marrying out of our country and our faith. Now that he is established in the United States it is fitting and proper for him to choose an American as his bride. As long as he makes the right choice. I believe he has done that. I hope you agree that he is worthy of you and you are worthy of him."

Emily struggled to say something besides yes, but he held up his hand and continued talking.

"I know you don't love him," he said.

Emily choked on her tea.

"Don't protest. It's not important. It doesn't matter. What matters is that I believe you can learn to love him."

Emily felt her eyes fill with tears. Yes, she wanted to say, I can learn to love him, I've been practicing for three years, but can he learn to love me? The answer was a resounding no.

"He may seem cool and distant and businesslike," his father continued. "But underneath he has a warm and compassionate nature. And once you are married he will be able to relax and have a normal family life. All those women parading through his life… It wasn't right. I told him it wasn't conducive to a lasting relationship. Finally he saw I was right."

Emily opened her mouth to protest, to say something, anything, but the older man held up his hand, palm forward.

"I realize now all those women served a purpose. And that was to show him how to appreciate what true value is in a woman. How to look beyond the superficial for inner beauty."

Emily knew he was saying these things to reassure her, to tell her that she didn't need to worry about competing with all those glamorous women in Ben's past, but in fact it had the opposite effect. At that moment, just as Emily wished she could fall through a trap door and disappear, Ben came in the door. Surprised to see his father and his fiancée having tea in his office, he braced his hands against the dark woodwork and surveyed them with raised eyebrows.

"We were just talking about you," his father explained.

"That's what I was afraid of," Ben said. "What did you say about me?"

"That though Emily may be put off by your cool exterior, underneath beats a warm, loving heart."

Emily could have sworn that Ben's ears turned red. But he quickly took control of the conversation.

"Thank you, Father. I'm sure Emily was glad to hear that piece of good news. Unfortunately she knows me better than anyone. She's put up with me through the worst and the best of times here at the office. And she knows exactly what she's getting in for, don't you, Emily?" he asked, and walked across the floor to place his hands on her shoulders.

"Yes, of course," she said dutifully. It was all for show, she told herself. To show his father he was making an effort to make this marriage succeed. The warmth of his hands on her shoulders made her want to rest her cheek against his hand, made her want to believe that love *can* follow marriage, though she knew in his case it wouldn't. If he was ever going to love her, he would love her by now.

After all, they'd worked together for three years. Through the worst and best of times, just as he said.

"That's not all I have to say, Son," the old Sheik said. "I want to tell you how happy I am you have chosen Emily for your bride. I couldn't have done better myself. She's everything you need to make your life complete. You have my blessing. Just one thing. I know Emily is an important member of your staff..."

"Important? She's the only one I could never get along without!"

"Yes, yes, I understand, but is that where you want your wife to be, in your office instead of your home? What about children, what will you do when—"

"Let me worry about that, Father," Ben said brusquely.

Emily pressed her lips together to keep from blurting out the truth. That there would be no children. That she would be a wife in name only. Let *him* worry about it. That was easy for him to say. As if she, too, wasn't worried sick about the outcome of this sham marriage.

The truth was, her worries didn't count. She had no say at all in this marriage. If Ben wanted her to continue working, she would. If he wanted her to stay home, she'd do that. It was only for a year. After that she'd get her life back.

Emily couldn't see the expression on Ben's face since he was still standing behind her, but she could imagine how he looked. Upset with his father. Worried and perhaps a little guilty for putting one over on his father. Or was his father so sure of his theory that love follows marriage that he was putting one over on Ben?

Emily made excuses for not having dinner with Ben's family, who were all staying with him. She had too much to do. Besides confirming their hotel reservations, she had to call the photographer, the caterer and the musicians. The next night she had to attend a bridal shower that the garden club was throwing for her.

The following evening she didn't know if it was a conspiracy or just a normal bridal shower, but most of the gifts were in the form of lacy lingerie. She opened package after package to find a plum-colored teddy, a pale pink camisole, a long white nightgown with spaghetti straps. Shrieks and cries filled the air at the home of her friend Sheila. She was famous for her tea roses, so named because they often smelled of tea or fresh fruit.

"Wait till Ben sees you in that," Mary Lynn said, grinning as she held up a sheer nightie.

Emily managed to smile, but there was a knot inside her chest that had been growing since the day she'd agreed to be Ben's wife. Tonight it threatened to rise up and choke her. By the end of the evening she was near tears. All this beautiful lingerie, and it would all go to waste. Even if Ben saw her in it, it wouldn't mean a thing to him. Not after all the women who'd paraded through his life—in or out of clothes.

She let her friends think her weepy state was because she was so touched by their thoughtfulness. That was partly true. The other part was the shame she felt letting them think that her boss wanted to marry her because he loved her. She dreaded the thought of telling them in a year that the sexy garments they'd showered her with were still in their boxes, still unworn. And the marriage was all over.

It was her last night in her house. She had packed most everything into cardboard boxes. The house seemed forlorn and lonely, and so did Emily. After growing up in a large, noisy family, she'd treasured her privacy. But tonight privacy was the last thing she wanted. There was a hollow feeling in her chest. She'd heard of last-minute jitters, but she didn't feel jittery; she felt sad. Sad that she wasn't getting married for the usual reasons. Sad that she'd fallen in love with someone so far out of her reach.

If she hadn't given her word to Ben, if his whole family hadn't assembled to witness the ceremony tomorrow, as well as her best friends, she'd be tempted to flee. When the phone rang, she reached for it in the dark. There was only one person who could be calling her. Her heart lurched. His voice was dark and deep and somehow soothing.

"Hello, Ben."

"I've forgotten. What time am I to arrive at the church?"

"One o'clock. The wedding is at two."

"That's right," he said. There was a long silence on his part. In the background was loud music and laughter. At least he wasn't lonely on the eve of his wedding.

"What's going on?" she asked.

"It's my family. They've started celebrating a little early. Weddings are very important in our culture."

"I see," she said. Not for the first time she wondered if she should have told her family. Then she wouldn't be alone tonight. They'd be there, laughing and talking and making music, too. And celebrating. Celebrating what? How could she invite them and let them think this was a real wedding. She knew what they'd say when they met Ben.

A real honest-to-God sheik.

You've been holding out on us, Emily, girl.

We knew you'd surprise us one of these days and do something unexpected.

"Then they don't suspect," she asked.

"There's nothing to suspect. I've been honest with them. I've told them we don't love each other, but that we're giving the marriage a year. They have no doubt we'll learn to love each other. When it doesn't work out the way they hope, they can't say we didn't try."

But Emily knew perfectly well Ben was not going to try. He wasn't going to try to love her, he wasn't going to try to make their marriage work. As for her, she *was* going to try. Try to keep her love a secret. To hide it from the world. So far she'd been successful. But she'd only worked with him. Now she had to live with him. She would have to be vigilant. Walk a tightrope. Try to look happily married but not wildly in love. What if she couldn't do it? What if people guessed? Peggy, for example. Or even Ben.

"Are you sure you want to go through with this, Ben?" she asked. Maybe, just maybe it wasn't too late to call it off.

"Of course," he said. "Don't you?"

"Of course. I just wondered…"

"Last-minute jitters?"

"Maybe," she admitted.

"It's the wedding. All the hoopla. Maybe you were right in not inviting your family. In any case, I'll see you tomorrow. I understand it's bad luck for me to see you before the ceremony. So, until then…goodnight."

His voice was so seductive it made shivers go up her spine. And he didn't even know it. He didn't know the effect he had on her. Thank heavens for that. She breathed a sigh of relief and dropped the phone into the cradle. Then she pulled the blankets up around her ears as if she could hide. But there was no hiding. Tomorrow was now, she noted with a glance at the clock. It was past midnight, and it was her wedding day. Already. Her dress hung in the closet, pale shimmering organza, just waiting to make an appearance. Waiting to knock their eyes out as she came down the aisle.

Sheila would be knocking on her door in a few hours to take her to the spa for a facial then to the hairdresser. She had to get some rest or she'd have huge circles under her eyes that no makeup artist could repair. But sleep did not come until morning.

She couldn't have done it without her friends. They took her to have a special mud wrap at the day-spa which left her face with a healthy glow. After the hairdresser, they whisked her to the little church in the suburbs in plenty of time to dress. By that time she was so rattled she could barely remember her own name, let alone where the church was. It wasn't Grace Cathedral or the Little Church of the Redwoods or the gothic church on the Stanford campus. They'd been booked years ahead. With only two weeks' notice, Emily was lucky to have found a small, frame church in a modest neighborhood that was free on this Saturday.

While the other members of the garden club transformed the humble chapel with the best and most beautiful pink and white roses from their gardens, the rest helped Emily get dressed. They fussed, they straightened, they smoothed and they fluffed her hair and touched up her makeup. There was no mirror in the small dressing room, so Emily had to be reassured that she looked her best by their broad smiles and by their exuberant cries of delight.

"Stunning."

"Gorgeous."

"Exquisite."

Her face flamed and her heart pounded as the hour grew near. Could they be right? Could she really look stunning, gorgeous and exquisite? Or were they referring to the dress? It didn't matter. She'd never looked stunning or gorgeous or exquisite or wanted to—all she'd ever wanted was to hide behind the scenes and let someone else be the star. But today she would have no choice. She was the bride, not the bridesmaid. All eyes would be on her. Her heart tripped a beat in her chest.

Mary Lynn and Georgia went out to check on the guests. They were back in minutes with their report. "We just met your fiancé, Emily, I mean your husband, husband-to-be. Oh, my!" Mary Lynn said.

"What's wrong?" Emily demanded.

"Nothing. I just didn't know. I mean Peggy told us, but I didn't believe he could be so gorgeous."

"Is he wearing…" Emily had never asked if he'd be in traditional dress or Western clothes.

"A tux. And the traditional sheik headdress. So is the best man. His brother, I suppose. But his father is in his robe. I can't believe this. It's like a fairy tale."

And, Emily thought, if anybody believed in fairy tales, they were heading for disappointment.

"I thought he looked a little nervous," Georgia said, "didn't you, Mary Lynn?"

"Definitely nervous. He asked several times if you were here, Emily. As if you wouldn't show on your wedding day."

Emily laughed nervously at the absurdity of the idea. But she hadn't walked down the aisle yet. Peggy's husband, Bud, was waiting to escort her, in lieu of her own father, but though she heard the organist tuning up, she wasn't ready. She realized she would never be really ready. Never in a hundred years would she be ready to be the bride of Sheik Ben Ali. It was wrong, all wrong, and she suspected Ben knew it, too. That's why he looked nervous.

There was a timid knock on the door of the small anteroom. It was Ben's mother dressed in a trailing blue robe of the finest silk. She hugged Emily and presented her with a pearl-and-diamond necklace, which she said could also be worn as a tiara. In halting English she explained it was a family heirloom to be worn on the bride's wedding day and other festive occasions and handed down to future generations. Emily was stunned by her generosity. Her first impulse was to refuse the gift. But to refuse would have hurt her feelings. As his mother helped her fasten it around her neck, she resolved to give it back to Ben. He would understand that she couldn't keep it.

By accepting the gift and sliding the clasp in place, Emily knew there was no turning back. Wrong or right, she was going through with the charade. With the help of a friend on each side, she made it to the back of the church. They covered her face with the veil. The music began. She tucked her hand into Bud's arm and they began the long walk down the aisle to the altar. All heads turned in her direction. A sea of faces swam in front of her. A collective gasp filled the church. She was only half-aware of the voices.

"Isn't she beautiful?"

"Lovely."

"A beautiful bride."

"Ravishing."

"Radiant."

They weren't just being polite. She could tell. The ugly duckling had become a swan just in time for her own wedding. She held her head high and breathed evenly. And accepted her new role. No longer in the background, no longer the worker bee, today, for the first time in her life, she was the queen, or if not the queen, at least a princess. The star of the show. She squared her shoulders and looked straight ahead. She felt beautiful. Ravishing, radiant. It was a heady feeling. One that wouldn't last, but one she would never forget.

Ben stood stiffly, his hands clenched at his sides as he watched Emily come down the aisle. To say he was stunned was putting it mildly. Though he couldn't see her face very well, he could see the lace bodice molded to her breasts, her slim waist and the billowing organza skirt. He could hear the murmurs, smell the roses and hear the music. He was getting married. He was almost thirty-five and he was getting married for the first and the last time.

No matter what happened, he could never go through this again. He felt as if a door had closed on his past life and another one had just opened. Ahead of him was the unknown. But this woman, this stranger, was going with him into the great unknown. His eyes were fastened on Emily, but he was aware of his family, his father and his mother, his sisters, brothers, nieces and nephews all beaming their approval.

He felt a surge of energy flow through him. His whole being was suffused with a feeling of joy. He was fulfilling his destiny, as a man, as a son and as a husband. He understood the value of tradition, he'd been brought up with it, but it wasn't until today that he felt a part of the ongoing pageant.

Emily came to the altar, the minister stepped forward and asked him if he would love, honor and obey her. His gaze locked on to Emily's. She was looking at him expectantly. Waiting. The whole church was waiting. The whole world was waiting for Sheik Ben Ali to answer. The lights in the church dimmed and the crowd faded away, and suddenly he and Emily were the only two people in the world. The only two who counted. He took a deep breath.

"I will," he said.

Then it was Emily's turn to promise to love, honor and obey him. Till death parted them. He knew she didn't mean it, any more than he meant what he'd said, but she must have inherited some of her family's acting ability, because the look in her eyes said she meant every word. And that she trusted him. He was determined to be worthy of that trust. She looked so vulnerable standing there with her hand in his, her gray eyes wide and trusting. Yet he knew she was strong. Strong, but vulnerable, too. It made him want to see to it that no one ever hurt her.

She was never good at hiding her feelings. He always knew when she didn't like one of his ideas. Or disagreed with him on a proposal. He wanted to take her hands in his, to assure her everything would be all right. But how did he know? From now on, this was uncharted territory, for both of them.

When it came time to kiss the bride, her bridesmaid lifted her veil and he drew in a sharp breath. How was it she could have hidden her beauty all these years? How could he not have guessed that under those baggy clothes, under her modest demeanor and behind her glasses, there was a beautiful person underneath? Not just beautiful but with an innocent sensuality that simmered beneath the surface, just waiting to be awakened.

She lifted her face toward his and closed her eyes and waited for his perfunctory kiss. He meant to brush her lips with his, but something happened in the space of a brief moment. He forgot his good intentions. He forgot this was Emily, his longtime, loyal assistant. The woman who faced him was now his wife, and he felt a powerful need to claim her in front of God and these witnesses. He lowered his head and kissed her with a hunger that shocked and surprised him. And her.

Her lips, at first stiff and unresponsive, softened under the pressure of his kiss. He felt the shock waves ripple through her body then he heard her heart beating in time to his. If they hadn't been in a church, standing in front of a hundred people or more, he might have kissed her again. Her eyes flew open. She teetered backward on her heels. He took her arm in his and steadied her. The crowd oohed and aahed, and they walked down the aisle holding hands tightly and smiling at the crowd. Her hand was like ice. Either she was in a state of shock from his kiss or she was scared silly.

Then there were pictures, pictures with his family and pictures with her friends. And next the reception at a lovely hotel ballroom they were lucky enough to get on such short notice. A string trio played in the background. Black-jacketed waiters passed trays of lavish hors d'oeuvres, champagne and sparkling cider. Though Ben drank alcohol moderately, he was sensitive to the desires of his Muslim relatives who would abstain.

He didn't see much of Emily during the reception. He didn't know if she was purposely avoiding him or it was just chance. After he'd introduced her to his family, she was taken aside by his mother and sister for what he supposed was a heart-to-heart chat, perhaps warning her of his personality quirks, as if she didn't know. He took the opportunity to speak to the ladies of the garden club. To thank them for the flowers.

"We're going to miss her," Peggy said, wiping a tear from her eye.

"She'll just be across town," Ben said. "You can have your meetings at my apartment. On the terrace."

Mary Lynn blinked back a tear. "But it won't be the same."

No, it wouldn't be the same. Nothing would be the same. Not in his life or in hers. Would she miss her friends, her garden and her club? Would he miss the peace and the tranquility of having a place of his own? Would she miss having her privacy as much as he would? Would she ask him where he was going and when he was coming home? Would she get homesick and sneak back to her house? Ben insisted she retain it, and he was paying the rent on it. How she explained that to her friends, he didn't know. He just knew it would make a smoother transition when the year was up.

The guests finally left, after receiving the traditional small net bags of sugar-coated almonds that signified good luck. In a suite they'd reserved upstairs, Ben changed into gray slacks, a casual shirt and a sweater, while Emily changed her clothes in the adjoining room with the help of his mother and sisters.

Ben's mother kissed and hugged Emily and told her she was like another daughter to her. She begged her to take good care of Ben, which made Ben shake his head. He'd been on his own for fifteen years, and now they wanted Emily to take care of him. Their tears flowed copiously as they said goodbye. The family planned to stay at Ben's place during the honeymoon but would be gone when the couple returned from the San Juan Islands in Puget Sound.

But the plane didn't take off. They sat in their spacious first-class seats for an hour before the announcement came that they were having engine trouble and the airline was sending another plane to take them to Seattle.

"You look tired," Ben said, noting that Emily had tilted her head back and closed her eyes. "We'll stay here overnight and take the first plane out tomorrow. Come on," he said, taking her arm with one hand and her overnight bag with the other. "Let's go back to the hotel."

The hotel was more than happy to oblige with the bridal suite. The only trouble was there was only one bed in the bridal suite. Never mind that it was big enough for a family of four, there was still only one. And they were two. Two people, who, while legally married, were not eager to sleep in the same bed.

"You take the bed," Ben said. "I'll push the chairs together and—"

''No, you won't. I'm shorter than you are. I can curl up in a chair and—''

''Emily, you just promised to love and obey me.''

Emily's face turned red. Maybe he shouldn't have reminded her, but he didn't want to argue any longer over something so trivial.

''No decent man would take the bed while his wife slept in a chair,'' he explained.

She bit her lip and nodded her consent. What else could she do when he reminded her of her vows? Of course, Ben didn't know it, but it wasn't the part about obeying that bothered her, it was the part about loving him. She grabbed her small bag and took refuge in the bathroom. She'd meant to pack her granny gown, but Peggy had taken over the packing at the last minute, and the granny gown was nowhere to be seen. Fortunately the nightgown with the spaghetti straps came with a matching robe, otherwise Emily didn't know what she would have done—hidden in the bathroom until he'd turned the lights out, then raced across the room and dived under the covers?

Instead she took a long bath in the huge tub that was built for two, and then dressed in her new silky lingerie. She stared at herself in the mirror. Who was that stranger in the mirror? Could that shameless creature be her? The one with her cheeks still glowing, her eyes bright, wearing a silk nightgown that brushed sensuously against her skin? What would her family say if they could see her now? *What's gotten into you, Emily? Have you lost your mind completely? Where's your real nightgown? Or what about your cotton pj's? You're not the filmy lingerie type, you know.*

Coming back down the aisle today to the sound of the organ playing the processional, with all those people watching her, smiling at her, she wished they'd been there. She wished they could have seen her, wished she could have seen the astounded expressions on their faces and shared the moment with them.

She took a deep breath, opened the door and walked calmly and quietly across the thick carpet of the spacious bridal suite, with its antique white-and-gold furniture, as if it was the most normal thing in the world for her to be spending the night with her boss. Hopefully he had no idea that under the pale satin nightgown her heart was beating like a jungle drum. Goose bumps popped out all over her skin. She was cold, cold all over, from her head to her toes, and she would have made a mad dash for the warmth of the bed if there hadn't been a knock on the door.

Still fully dressed, Ben went to the door to allow room service to wheel in a cart carrying a champagne bottle on ice, two long-stemmed glasses, a bowl of delectable fresh fruit, cheeses and assorted pastries.

"Did you order this?" Emily asked, eyeing the cart and forgetting her goal to hide under the covers.

"Compliments of the house," the waiter said. "It comes with the suite. Newlywed special." He winked, Ben tipped him and the waiter backed out the door.

"Are you hungry?" Ben asked, lifting the champagne bottle out of the ice bucket. For the first time since they left the reception she noticed what he was wearing. That's how distracted she'd been. She finally took a good look and noticed his classic polo shirt unbuttoned partway so the crisp dark hair on his chest was plainly visible. She realized that in all the time she'd known him she'd never seen him in anything but a business suit or a tux. And now this. And what would be next?

Her heart fluttered, and she dragged her gaze away. It occurred to her she might see a whole lot more of him before this honeymoon was over, and if she couldn't control her newly awakened libido, she was in for big trouble.

Hungry? She shook her head. She couldn't think about food. All she could do was worry about how much more she was going to see of her husband. First he'd unbuttoned his shirt, next he might take it off. Then what would she do? There was just so much stimulation she could take without crumbling.

On the other hand, he hadn't given her nightgown a second glance, so clearly this was not a problem for him. Of course not. To him she was only his assistant. Or at best a friend who was doing him a favor. Which was in itself a big step from his employee. She didn't mind being his friend. She did mind being his wife. It was a bigger adjustment than she'd thought.

"I am," he said. "I didn't get a chance to eat at the reception. Too busy talking." He pulled out a chair at the small table by the window. "At least keep me company."

She sat down without another word. She didn't want to be accused again of not obeying him. Besides, she didn't have the strength to protest, even when he poured two glasses of champagne and filled two plates with strawberries and Brie cheese and crackers and set one in front of her.

"What did you think of the wedding?" he asked in between bites.

She took a sip of champagne. "It was nice."

"Nice? Is that all you can say?"

"The church looked beautiful, I know that much. But I'm afraid I was too nervous to remember much more than that." Except for the kiss. She remembered that. She was afraid he was going to mention it. The kiss that shocked and surprised her. Whatever possessed him to kiss her like that in front of everyone? Or in front of no one, for that matter. It was totally out of character. Totally out of place in a marriage like theirs. Unless it was the custom in his country. She wanted to know, but she wasn't going to ask him. Never. He'd probably forgotten it by now. But she hadn't.

"The church looked beautiful, but you looked even more beautiful," he said.

He sounded sincere, but the compliment flowed so smoothly from his lips she couldn't help but wonder if he meant it.

"The necklace I wore was a gift from your mother. It's a family heirloom. She asked that I pass it on to the next generation. Of course I'll give it back to you. I can't keep it."

"Why not?"

"Because there won't be a next generation. I mean…"

"I know what you mean," he said. "I, too, have a present for you. One you can keep."

"Oh, no. I didn't get you anything. I didn't know… I mean I've never been married before." She was babbling like an idiot. Of course she hadn't been married before. He knew that. Everyone knew that.

"Don't worry about it. It's just a trinket. But something traditional in my culture." He got up and reached into his suitcase for a black jewelry case. "Come here," he said.

She crossed the room to sit on the edge of the bed, and he knelt in front of her and took her foot in his hand and stroked the arch of her foot.

She shivered, and at the same time a shaft of heat curled through her body. She had no idea the foot could be an erogenous zone. But when Ben touched her foot she felt sensations she'd never experienced before.

She looked down to see him take a delicate silver ankle bracelet from the box and fasten it around her ankle. He ran his finger around her ankle. "It fits," he said with satisfaction. "I thought it would."

"Thank you," she said in a choked voice, wishing he'd continue to stroke her foot and unable to take her eyes from the anklet.

"It's a custom for the groom to give the bride an ankle bracelet," he explained. "It's a symbol of their union. As long as she wears his anklet, she belongs to him."

"What a...a nice custom," she stammered. She wanted to say what was in her heart. That it was a beautiful custom. That she'd willingly wear his bracelet forever, till death parted them. But that would scare him and send him packing before they'd even had a honeymoon. Not that she wanted to have a honeymoon, but...

"Your family is charming," she said to break the silence. Ben continued to kneel on the floor with her foot in his hand, causing minor tremors to rock her body.

"They're very fond of you." He got to his feet at last. "I almost wish...it might be easier if..."

"Yes?"

"Nothing. I'm afraid they're going to be disappointed when our marriage comes to an end. Perhaps you were right in not telling your family."

"I know I was. You can't imagine how they'd react. They're so emotional. They wear their hearts on their sleeves and get carried away by the slightest thing. And they're so anxious, so worried about me."

"*They're* worried about *you?*"

"Yes, it's ridiculous. I'm the only one who finished college. The only one with a steady job. But that kind of thing isn't important to them. They're forever talking to me about finding myself, urging me to express myself. For them, that's what counts."

"But you do express yourself. In your work, in your garden."

"Thank you. I wish they could hear you say that."

"They could if I could meet them sometime."

Emily shook her head vehemently, and her silky robe slid off one shoulder. She could just see it now, her crazy family discovering she was married. To a sheik. They'd be all over him like glue. Demanding to know when he'd fallen in love with their serious, sedate, sensible sister, daughter, whatever. Asking to see his ceremonial robes, asking if he trained falcons and rode horseback and wanting to hear all about his country, his family and his life in general.

"I don't mean to tell them we're married," Ben explained. "Just bring them up to the office, and I'll set them straight about you. I don't think they appreciate all your qualities." It may have been an accident, but just at that moment, his dark gaze dropped to the neckline of her nightgown. At that moment his expression changed. His jaw tightened and the muscle in his temple jumped.

Her pale, exposed skin prickled with awareness. His gaze was like a caress. She felt it to the tips of her bare toes. She tried to think of something to say. To draw his attention elsewhere, but her brain wasn't working right. It wasn't working at all. Her senses, however, were definitely on full alert. Alert to his hooded gaze that was glued to the bodice of her nightgown. Stripping it away with his eyes, as surely as he might have removed it with his hands. She felt her nipples pucker under his heated gaze.

Ever so casually she drew her robe up over her shoulders, and he jerked his eyes away. He stood abruptly and looked down at her. "It's late, Emily," he said with an unexpected harsh note in his voice. "Go to bed."

It didn't take more urging for her to follow that order.

Leaving a half glass of champagne on the table, she got into bed—robe, nightgown and all—and pulled the blanket up to her chin. From this safe place she watched him turn the lights down and disappear into the bathroom with his shaving kit. She closed her eyes so she wouldn't see what he was wearing when he returned to the room. But there was nothing she could do to keep from imagining a bare chest, long muscular legs and broad shoulders.

She heard the sound of the shower running. Now her imagination really kicked into high gear. In her mind's eye she saw soapsuds caught in the hair on his chest. Shampoo running down his back. Water cascading down his washboard stomach to the apex of his thighs. She pressed her face into the pillow and stifled a moan. How long would this go on?

One horrible thought came to her. What if they'd been given the honeymoon suite at the resort? She couldn't go through another night like this. What was so bad about it? For one thing, though they were not sleeping in the same bed, she was painfully aware of his presence. If she'd only known how difficult marriage to Ben would be, she would have said no when he suggested it. For him, this intimacy meant nothing. But to her, every word, every touch left an indelible mark on her consciousness. That's why she asked for a cottage with two bedrooms at the island hotel and deliberately didn't tell them that they were newlyweds.

She heard his footsteps as he came out of the steamy bathroom and walked across the floor. She smelled his soap and shampoo. It occurred to her he might be wearing nothing but a towel. Frustrated beyond belief and overwhelmed with curiosity, she turned over and opened her eyes.

Chapter Five

"I thought you were asleep," he said. He *was* wearing a towel, and only a towel. If she hadn't been lying down, she would have fallen down. The sight of him with a towel casually knotted around his waist was even more disturbing than she'd imagined. He seemed completely unaware of her reaction. Of her throbbing pulse and pounding heart. As if this was a usual thing to spend the night with a woman and appear half-dressed from the shower. For him it probably was.

She struggled to keep her eyes on his face and not let her gaze drift downward. She wouldn't let herself imagine what would come next.

"I can't sleep knowing you're going to sit in a chair all night," she said.

"All right, you take the chair," he said.

She looked at the chair. If she were wearing the old granny gown she'd left behind packed in a cardboard box in her house, she would have taken him up on it. Leaped out of bed and grabbed a blanket and given him the bed.

But she was not going to parade around the room again in the ensemble she was currently wearing. She supposed Peggy had packed the flimsy gown because it was the kind of thing you're supposed to wear on your honeymoon. But not this honeymoon.

This was the kind of honeymoon where the bride wore a flannel granny gown and slept in a separate bed. A separate room would be preferable. She racked her brain to recreate the conversation she'd had with the reservations clerk regarding the accommodations at the inn on Orcas Island, but it had all happened so fast. While she'd been on the phone to the inn, the photographer was on the other line. But she knew, she was sure, she'd insisted on the two-bedroom cottage.

Ben stood in the middle of the room watching her, hoping she'd get out of the bed so he could get another look at that nightgown or more accurately, her body inside the nightgown. He'd only had a tantalizing glimpse of creamy white skin, the swell of small but perfect breasts and one bare shoulder. Just enough to drive a man crazy. This was his wedding night. Was it wrong to want to see more of your bride than just a glimpse?

Was it wrong to want more than just a kiss at the altar? Not that he was going to make love to her. They'd already decided against that. About that kiss…she'd never mentioned it and neither did he. Maybe she chalked it up to male chauvinism. To some kind of primitive need to claim his bride. And maybe that's all it was. Or maybe she'd decided it was the tension building until it exploded at the altar. Which made sense to him.

The problem was that he couldn't forget it. He kept wanting to kiss her again. To see if it would have the same effect on him. To see if it would have the same effect on her. To see if the first time was a fluke.

"Well?" he asked.

"I...uh...think I'll stay here. If you promise not to tell anyone."

"Don't worry," he said as his lips twisted in a wry smile. "I'm not likely to."

Needless to say, Ben didn't sleep well in the chair. He tried every position he could think of, folding his legs at the knees, draping his arms over the padded arms of the chair. But nothing worked. It wasn't just physical discomfort. He'd slept like a baby on a carpet in a desert tent more than once.

Tonight his problem was mental, as well. He couldn't get over the fact that this was his wedding night and he wasn't making love to his wife. He knew it wasn't possible, he knew it wasn't going to happen, he'd known for weeks, but his body hadn't gotten the message. His body was hot and throbbing. His body was telling him he shouldn't be sleeping alone. Not tonight.

He got up and walked around the room. He opened the window, but it didn't help cool his libido. He stood watching Emily's tousled hair and her pale cheek against the pillow and listening to her soft, regular breathing indicating she was sleeping peacefully. Why shouldn't she? She had a huge superking-size bed to herself. Which she was only taking up one-third of at most.

He stared at her for a long time before he eased himself under the covers on the far side of the bed. He let out a sigh of relief as he stretched his legs out for the first time under the smooth cotton sheets. He noted with relief that Emily hadn't budged. He closed his eyes so he wouldn't see her bare shoulder or her soft curls, but her scent wafted across the bed and filled his senses and caused his body to tense. He reminded himself she was his bride legally, but not really. He still couldn't sleep. Not until dawn.

The next morning Emily snuggled under the covers and smiled to herself. She'd had the most incredible dream in which she'd gotten married to Ben and afterward made mad passionate love to him in a huge bed in a hotel room. When she opened her eyes she was disoriented. The pale wallpaper, the elegant furniture and the empty champagne bottle on the table, the sun streaming in the window. Where was she? She felt not one ring but two on the third finger of her left hand.

She turned her head and clamped her lips together to keep from screaming. Ben was sleeping next to her. Ben, her husband. It all came back to her in a flood of confusing images and mixed feelings. For a long moment she studied his face. She'd seen him angry, upset, excited and happy, but she'd never seen him in repose, his face relaxed, his dark hair in disarray, the faint worry lines in his forehead gone.

Without thinking she impulsively reached over and brushed his hair out of his eyes. Without warning he reached for her hand and grabbed it.

This time she did scream. He put one hand over her mouth and the other around her waist. He turned on his side and pulled her tight against his hard chest.

"You frightened me. What are you doing here?" she demanded, her voice muffled against his hand. He removed his hand from her mouth, but kept her pinned against him. She had no idea what he was or wasn't wearing under the sheets. And she was terrified she was going to find out. "I thought you were sleeping," she said.

"I *was* sleeping, until you woke me up," he explained, his eyes narrowed and dangerously dark.

"I'm sorry, but I thought you were sleeping on the chair." She was trying desperately to sound normal, as normal as she could with her breasts pressed against his chest,

his legs dangerously close to hers. She tried to wriggle out
of his grasp, but he had her in a viselike grip. She had to
put some space between them. She placed her palm on his
bare chest to push him away, but it didn't work that way.
Instead her hand was caught between them. When her fingers chanced on his male nipple it hardened beneath her
touch. He tensed and drew a sharp breath. Amazed at her
power to cause such a reaction, Emily moved her hand to
feel the muscles and the sinews of his broad chest.

"If you keep on like that, I won't be responsible for what
happens," he muttered, his jaw clenched tight.

Shocked at his words and knowing he meant them, she
finally wrenched herself out of his arms and tossed the
blankets off the bed. Without looking back she grabbed her
suitcase and raced to the bathroom.

He followed her and shouted through the door. "Our
plane is at ten."

"I'll be ready," she assured him.

She was ready, as far as her outward appearance. Once
again she donned her lightweight wool pantsuit, purchased
especially for her honeymoon, which was one size smaller
than she usually wore and fit her perfectly, her new contact
lenses, and went to the airport with her new husband. That
was how she looked outwardly. Inwardly she was a bundle
of nerves. Counting the days until they could return to the
city, return to work, return to normal. Of course, she
wouldn't really breathe normally until the end of this year
when this sham marriage would be over.

This time the plane took off without incident. And without incident they stepped into a rental car at the Seattle-
Tacoma Airport and drove three hours to the ferry boat that
would take them to the San Juan Islands. From time to time
along the way she stole a glance at Ben. She had to admit

he was gorgeous in his Shetland wool sweater and khaki pants. How strange to see him in casual clothes. Which reminded her she'd almost seen him in no clothes at all. Her face flamed at the memory and she turned to look out the window, but saw only her own reflection in the glass.

She also had to admit that she had a few regrets about that morning. One was that she'd never know what he wore to bed, if anything. Because from now on they'd have separate bedrooms. Both during this so-called honeymoon and after they went back to live at Ben's. And the other regret was that she hadn't stayed just a moment longer in that bed. Just to see what would happen. It might have been her last chance. No, it definitely was her last chance. Just when she'd gotten up her nerve to tentatively explore his body, she'd lost it.

Ben drove the small rental sports car with his usual speed and competence toward the ferry landing. But while he drove he wondered what he was doing going on a honeymoon. Why in the hell had he ever mentioned it? Because it was expected. Because it was the custom. But he could have easily said they had no time, they couldn't both be gone from the office at the same time, or he didn't believe in honeymoons. If last night was an example of how they would spend the next six nights, in frustration and longing for something that wasn't going to happen, he was ready to cancel right now.

He glanced at Emily. She was looking out the window at the blue-green waters of Puget Sound as casually as if she took a honeymoon trip every weekend. Her hasty departure from the bed this morning told him just how little she'd enjoyed the experience of sharing a brief embrace. She obviously had no idea how it affected him to have her soft hand rub across his bare chest. His body was still throbbing with unfulfilled lust.

He was ashamed to say it, he was ashamed to even think it—but it was true. He was lusting after his assistant. The woman whose business skills made him the envy of every other CEO in town. Now, after working with her for three years, he just realized she had other skills he'd never known about. Skills that she herself was unaware of, which made her more desirable than all the other women he'd dated. That didn't make it right. He'd told her in no uncertain terms this marriage didn't involve sex and he meant it. Or rather he'd meant it at the time. Maybe they should have discussed it instead of dismissing it so quickly.

Maybe it wasn't too late. He sneaked another glance at her, noting her profile, the soft outline of her cheek and her stubborn little chin.

"Tell me more about the San Juan Islands," he said to break the silence. "Why are we going there?"

"They're supposed to be beautiful, and I've always wanted to go there. In the brochure the hotel sent me they mention the quiet, the feeling of isolation, the water all around you and the clear, cool air. On Orcas Island there aren't even any stop signs."

"What are we going to do there?" he asked. Since he knew they weren't going to stay in their room until noon making mad, passionate love every day, she'd better have something else in mind.

She did. She mentioned sailing, kayaking, hiking, clamming.

"What about our accommodations at the, uh…"

"At the Orcas Island Inn?"

"Ah, yes, the Orcas Island Inn." Damned if he could remember where they were staying. He'd left that and everything else up to her. She'd made all the arrangements.

She was good at it. She'd been making his travel arrangements for the past three years. But she'd never gone anywhere with him before.

"The resort is on thirty acres with an old mansion as the main lodge. It looked beautiful, but I asked for a two-bedroom cottage with an ocean view. I thought that would be the best for us, considering..." She cleared her throat and turned to look out the window again as if she couldn't bear to finish her sentence.

"Considering we're not sleeping together."

"Yes."

"So you didn't mention we're on our honeymoon."

"Oh, no. You saw what happened back there at the hotel. They're apt to bring in baskets of fruit and buckets of champagne. I thought you wouldn't want anyone to fuss. I know I don't."

"Right."

"You know how everyone looks at honeymooners."

"No," he said, faking an innocent tone. "How do they look at them?"

"Well, like they...they, you know, they smirk at them or something."

"We wouldn't want that," he said, smothering a smile. "That might make us the center of attention."

She gave a little shudder of apprehension, just as he knew she would.

"Was it so bad, being the center of attention at the wedding? Having all those heads turn, hearing everyone say how beautiful you looked?"

"Yes, no, I don't know. Let's say I enjoyed it at the moment, but I was relieved when it was over. I wasn't born to be in the spotlight. But I'm glad I had a chance to see what it was like. It wasn't as bad as I thought it would be. As for looking beautiful, they say *that* no matter what you look like. Cruella DeVille could walk down the aisle and you'd still see everyone nudge each other and say, 'Doesn't she look beautiful?'"

He shook his head. It was useless to argue with her. No matter how she looked, she'd always feel like the ugly duckling in a family of swans. Unless he could convince her otherwise. But it would take more than words. It would take patience and understanding. It would take time. It would take just the right strokes, both physical and mental. It would be a challenge. One that intrigued him. One he couldn't turn his back on.

Once on board the green-and-white car ferry bound for Orcas Island, they stood elbow to elbow on the deck watching great blue herons skim the surface of the water. Cool breezes blew through the narrow channel as they passed several small, thickly wooded islands.

"How about some coffee?" he asked.

"Sure."

He walked into the large lounge toward the coffee bar, but once inside, he stopped and made a call from his cell phone. Then he bought the coffee and took it out to Emily. A half hour later the venerable old ferry docked and they drove their car off into the mist along Horseshoe Highway, bending around Eastsound village until they reached the thirty-acre complex.

The lavish mansion, now the main lodge of the most luxurious retreat in the San Juans, was charming with its fourteen-inch-thick walls and windows made from porthole glass nearly an inch thick. Before they checked in they admired the fireplace in the dining room set with marble left over from the building of the Nebraska.

However lovely the mansion, Emily was glad she'd chosen the cottage accommodations overlooking the water. She was until the reservation clerk told her she had reserved a one-bedroom and not a suite.

"But I'm sure I said two-bedroom," she insisted.

"I'm so sorry," murmured the clerk.

"It doesn't matter," Ben said soothingly. "I'm sure we'll be perfectly comfortable...."

"I just hope they have a comfortable chair for you to sleep on," she said under her breath.

"Don't worry about me," he said with a friendly smile for the clerk.

"Don't forget the organ concert at five in the music room," the clerk said.

Emily smiled politely, but her heart sank when she saw the inside of the cottage. One small living room with two rustic chairs that flanked a stone fireplace. In the bedroom was one enormous feather bed covered with an old-fashioned canopy. Pendleton blankets with geometric designs were stacked on the end of the bed. The outside of the weathered wooden cottage was shrouded in shrubbery, except for the huge plate-glass windows overlooking the sound.

It had its own deck with two Adirondack chairs facing a magnificent view of boats and water and more islands. In short, it was perfect except for one thing. There was only *one* bedroom and *one* bed. There was also a small, well-appointed kitchenette finished in natural wood, with a microwave oven and a well-stocked refrigerator. A bottle of champagne with a ribbon around it and a basket of fresh fruit sat on the table. But not one chair big enough or comfortable enough for a six-foot-three-inch man to sleep in.

"Oh, no," Emily murmured after taking inventory.

"What's wrong?" asked Ben, walking into the kitchen from the bedroom where he was admiring the view from the picture window.

"You know what's wrong. There's been a terrible mistake. After I took such pains, after I deliberately…"

"You deliberately asked for two bedrooms, I know, but does it really matter?" he asked, putting his hand on her arm.

She jerked her arm away. "Of course it matters. Someone told them we were newlyweds." She didn't mean to sound cranky, but that's exactly how it came out.

"Who would do such a thing?" he asked.

"I don't know," she said shooting him a suspicious glance.

"Don't look at me," he said. "You're the one who made the reservations. Maybe they just guessed we're on our honeymoon by the way we look."

"We don't look like newlyweds," she said firmly. *Newlyweds can't tear their eyes away from each other. Newlyweds would be ripping each other's clothes off by now. Newlyweds would be under that canopy right now…*

"I don't know about that. You have a certain glow about you."

She shot him a lethal glance. She wasn't in the mood to be teased. She couldn't be glowing. She had nothing to glow about. Glowing or not, she couldn't face another night in close quarters with Ben. She had so little resistance. It would be so easy to make a fool of herself. If he touched her again, even by accident, if he tempted her by putting his arms around her, she might lose control of herself and throw herself at him. Fling herself into his arms. That would scare him all right. But it wasn't going to happen. Not if she had to bundle up and sleep on the deck.

"Come on, change your clothes," he said briskly. "We have time for a sail before the concert."

Needless to ask if he sailed. He did everything. And he did it perfectly. "I don't know how to sail," she said.

"I'll teach you."

"You go. I'll wait here." The perfect opportunity to be alone, to put some distance between them.

"Alone on our honeymoon?" he asked. "What would people say?"

"You wouldn't be gone long, would you? Besides, what do we care what people think? We don't know anyone here."

"Emily, we're going sailing."

She recognized that tone of voice. It was no use arguing when he sounded like that. She went into the bedroom and changed into a soft, new, stone-washed pair of jeans, a windbreaker and sneakers. When she came out he was at the door, one elbow propped against the door frame. His gaze flicked over her, and apparently she passed the test for what a novice sailor should wear, because he smiled and took her arm. She said a silent word of thanks to the garden club members who'd accompanied her on her clothes-shopping trips. If it weren't for them, she'd still be in her garden coveralls. In her other life she'd had suits for work and dungarees for after work. Period.

Down at the dock was a fleet of small sailboats for the use of the guests. The dock boy raised the sail on a small dinghy for them and handed them each a life jacket. Ben fastened his vest, but she was still fumbling with the ties on hers, so he did it for her.

"Where did you learn to sail?" she asked, trying to ignore the fact that his hands grazed her breasts and his face was inches from hers. He was so close she could smell his hair and see a small scar at the outer edge of his eyebrow. The extreme proximity didn't seem to bother him the way it did her. His hands were steady and tied the knots as if he'd been a sailor all his life.

"Our family has a place on the Gulf and my father taught

me when I was a boy. One summer he and I even built a small boat from a kit. I always thought someday I would…'' He tied the last knot but he didn't finish his sentence.

''But you don't sail on San Francisco Bay.''

''No, I've thought about it, but never wanted to take the time. But I'd like to. Maybe when we get back I'll look into getting a boat and joining the yacht club. It's a great sport, you'll see, you have the wind at your back and the sun in your eyes. I've missed it.''

He took her hand and helped her into the small craft. ''Stay aft, Emily,'' he said ''and man the rudder. You're the one who actually steers.''

''I am? I can't, I don't…''

''Yes you can. Three basic maneuvers are all you need to know. Sailing into the wind, sailing across the wind and sailing with the wind.'' He took her by the shoulders and sat her down in the rear of the small craft. Then he placed her hands around the tiller. ''When I tell you to, you pull the rudder in the opposite direction we want to go in.''

The dock boy shoved them off from the pier and suddenly they were on the slightly choppy waters of the Sound. While she sat at the rear, gripping the tiller in one hand and the edge of the boat in the other, Ben stood at the mast in the center of the boat, pulling on a rope to adjust the angle of the sail. When the sail caught the wind and sent the boat scudding forward, she felt the wind and the salt spray in her face. Ben grinned at her. A wave broke over the side of the boat and splashed her feet and sucked the breath from her lungs, but she grinned back. She couldn't help it. His enthusiasm was catching. Whether it was sailing or signing an agreement to bring in millions of dollars.

''How're you doing?'' he yelled.

''Fine. Nothing to it,'' she said sounding more confident

than she felt. He was having such a good time she couldn't bear to say she was scared and wet. Ben raised one thumb, and when she caught her breath she returned the gesture, though the cold breeze blew right through her jacket.

She thought she'd never seen Ben so happy. Not even when he'd culminated a big deal. A business transaction left him satisfied, but sailing excited and relaxed him at the same time, and she realized she'd have to encourage him to pursue it when they returned. As his assistant, she always felt free to offer her advice. Now as his wife, would she feel the same way? Or would she hesitate to interfere with his personal life? She realized he'd been working way too hard and it was partly her fault. She'd routinely overscheduled him. Not that he'd ever complained. On the contrary, he was ambitious and energetic and he...

"Duck," he yelled as the boom came swinging across the rear of the boat and hit her on the head. She blacked out for just a second, then came to, still clutching the tiller in her hands

"Emily," he yelled, leaping to her side as the boom swung crazily back and forth. "Are you all right?"

"Of course. I wasn't looking."

He studied her face. "You were off in another world."

How true. "Sorry."

"We'll turn back."

"No, don't do that. I'm fine. Really. And I think I'm catching on." Though her head was throbbing, she gave him her best attempt at a smile. She hated to cut short this outing, not when Ben was having such a good time.

He grabbed the boom and steadied it. "If you're sure..."

She nodded vigorously even as she felt a bump rising on the top of her head.

By the time they returned to the dock, she was soaked through, her head ached and her hands were numb. But she'd been sailing. She'd manned the tiller and avoided getting knocked down or thrown overboard.

Ben tied the boat to the dock and threw his arm over her shoulder the way he would a good pal. "That was great. You were great."

"Next time I'll be better. I'll pay attention."

"I almost forgot." He removed his arm from her shoulder and examined her face, running his thumb and forefinger over her forehead. He didn't mean it to be anything near a caress, she was sure of that, but her body didn't get the message. She was trembling all over and she couldn't catch her breath.

"What's wrong?" he asked.

"Nothing. I'm fine, I tell you."

"You're shaking like a leaf, and I can hear your heart beating from here." When his probing touch discovered the lump on her head, his eyebrows drew together in a frown. "Come on, we're getting back to the cabin." He drew her to his side and supported her with one arm around her waist all the way back. She knew she could make it on her own, but the feeling of being protected, cared for and looked after was too tempting to turn down. What was she going to do, wrench herself away and march back on her own?

They were no sooner inside the door of the cottage and he was stripping her jacket and sweater off her.

"Stop," she said. "That's enough." One more layer of clothes and he'd be down to her bare skin, to her new lace bra and panties. But he didn't listen. He hustled her into the luxurious bathroom with the claw-foot tub and turned on the hot water. Then he sat her on the commode and pulled off her shoes. Next he reached for the waistband of her jeans.

"Ben!"

"Really, Emily. What do you think I'm going to see that I've never seen before?"

He didn't need to remind her of his playboy past. She didn't need to be told that he was experienced beyond what she'd ever be. She stood, put her hands against his chest and shoved him out the door. The expression on his face was a combination of amusement and resignation.

"All right," he said. "I'm going. But if I don't hear from you every five minutes, I'm coming in to check. I can't risk having my assistant getting a concussion. I'm going to need every bit of your brain power to get us through the negotiations with Remsen Oil when we get back."

"Don't worry." She closed the door, shed her clothes and slid into the extralong, old-fashioned, porcelain tub. *His assistant. Her brain power. Negotiations.* She'd almost forgotten that she was his assistant first and foremost. And his wife in name only. If she didn't remember it, he'd be sure to keep reminding her. And if she didn't remember, she was going to get her heart broken.

She propped her feet on the edge of the tub, and the silver anklet gleamed, reminding her of what he'd said. That the anklet was a symbol, and as long as she wore it she belonged to him. Under the circumstances of their sham marriage, she should never have accepted it. He should never have offered it. It also reminded her of how he could reduce her to a quivering mass of sensations just by stroking her foot, just by bestowing a little gift on her. It meant nothing to him and, heaven help her, everything to her.

A few minutes later the bathroom door burst open and Ben walked in.

Chapter Six

Instinctively Emily gripped the edge of the porcelain and submerged herself in the steamy water—for what good it did her. Her whole body flushed and turned as red as a local lobster. Which she was sure he could plainly see from his angle. She wondered why she'd forgotten to lock the door. Was it because she secretly wanted him to come in?

"Are you all right? I've been calling you."

What was wrong with her?

It was the second time today she'd tuned out. The first time she'd almost been knocked silly, this time she was only in danger of mortal embarrassment.

"I'm fine," she gasped. "I'll be right out."

He left, but not before she saw him take a good long look at her naked body, his gaze lingering here and there at her most sensitive spots. She supposed he was curious. She supposed he was comparing her to the numerous shapely, big-busted model-like women he'd been familiar with in the past. She herself had made reservations for him and a companion for weekends here and there. She didn't like it, it hurt her like a knife in her chest, but she took pains not to let him know that. It was just part of her job. Now she was the one at the luxurious hotel with her boss. After all those years of feeling envious of his girlfriends, she now knew what it was like.

So this is what it felt like to be holed up with one of the city's most handsome and eligible bachelors. Former bachelor. It felt strange. It felt awkward. And it felt like she wished she could go home. The way he'd looked at her made her feel as if she was being evaluated. For what? Hadn't she proved herself over the years to be reliable, honest and faithful? It was almost as if…but no, there was to be no sex. That was the deal.

This time it was Emily who emerged from the bathroom clad only in a towel. This time it was Ben who couldn't tear his gaze away as she skittered down the hall on her way to the bedroom.

"Are you up to the organ concert?" he asked from the living room.

"Absolutely," she called as she stepped into a pair of bamboo-colored linen pants and pulled a long-sleeved, tab-collared tunic over her head. All these new clothes made her feel like a new woman. A woman she didn't know. A woman who wasn't quite what she used to be but wasn't what she was going to be, either. A woman on the edge, on the verge of some kind of scary breakthrough into another dimension of her personality.

Throwing aside her worries about where she'd sleep tonight, as well as how much of her Ben had really seen, she emerged from the bedroom with her face scrubbed clean of makeup and her hair in wispy tendrils around her face. She was anxious to get out of the cottage. An organ concert or whale watching, she didn't care what it was, just so it got them out. The last place she should be was in this charming honeymoon cottage with her new husband. The sooner they got out and mixed with other people, the better off they'd be. It was a bad idea to spend all this time with a husband who was a husband in name only. It made her want what she couldn't have. A real marriage and a real husband.

Ben looked up from the brochure he was reading in the cozy living room. "Be careful, Emily," he warned with a teasing smile. "You're glowing. People are going to talk."

Whether she wanted to or not, she *was* glowing, he decided. It wasn't just her face that was changing before his very eyes. It was her body and her new clothes. Where was the plain assistant who came to work in tailored suits that did nothing for her shapely little body? Inside those baggy skirts had been a lovely young woman trying to get out. One who didn't yet know how pretty she was, or how beautiful she could be. He planned to be the one to tell her and, even better, to show her. He'd like to begin tonight. Just the thought made his whole body go rigid. Picturing her as she got in touch with her sensual side made his smile widen.

"Don't be ridiculous," she said. But she blushed at his compliment, which was his intention.

Inside the music room the late-afternoon light streamed through a Belgian stained-glass clerestory. He watched Emily's eyes widen as she tilted her face to the windows. Her honest responses fascinated him. She was simply incapable of pretense. Her smile made him smile. She reacted to things as if she'd been in a cocoon for years. He wanted to keep the new experiences coming. Wanted to surprise her, dazzle her, impress her.

When the music from the giant aeolian organ with its two thousand pipes filled the room, he took her hand. She was so wrapped up in the Renaissance music she didn't appear to notice. He cast a glance at her profile. Noted her straight nose and her sweet mouth. He thought about the wedding kiss, and he leaned toward her, to brush her arm with his and to tighten his grip on her hand. She glanced at him, and the look of awareness in her eyes told him she wasn't completely immune to his touch.

He was determined to find out just how far he could go before the day was over. At the very least she might be receptive to another kiss. A longer, deeper kiss than at the wedding. And at the very most... His imagination went wild. The anticipation left his heart hammering. It had to be soon. It had to be tonight. He couldn't wait much longer.

After dinner in town at a highly recommended low-key local hangout where they dined on specialties of the region like wild mushroom soup and grilled salmon, they returned to the resort and strolled the grounds. He suggested returning to the cottage a number of times, but each time Emily thought of something she wanted to do, something she wanted to see like the indoor swimming pool or the stables or the game room. He almost thought she might be postponing their return to the room on purpose.

"Aren't you tired?" he asked her when she insisted on seeing the cozy, book-lined library.

She tried to say no, but he caught her hiding a yawn, and he insisted they go back to the cottage.

"If you're afraid I'll try to sleep in your bed again, don't be," he said as he unlocked the cottage door.

"It's your bed. We'll take turns. It's only fair."

"Then tonight is your turn," he said.

"Last night was my turn. Tonight I'll sleep on the floor."

He gave her a long look, noted the stubborn tilt of her chin and shrugged. In any negotiation, there were times when it was pointless to argue, and this was one of them. It was best to give in on this and save his clout for something more important. Something that would lead him

closer to his ultimate goal. Which, he realized with a moment of sudden clarity, was making love to his wife. It
sounded simple. It sounded like what they called a no-
brainer. But watching Emily walk past him into the bedroom with her head held high, he knew it wasn't going to
be.

It was going to be difficult. It was going to require tact
and diplomacy and all the charm he could muster. He'd
never really had to seduce other women. They all came
willingly. Some had even thrown themselves at him. Maybe
that was why Emily was such a challenge to him. Maybe
that was why he was so determined to make this a real
honeymoon. In every sense of the word.

He could have kicked himself for telling her there'd be
no sex in their relationship before he'd had a chance to
think it through. Now it would seem as though he was
going back on his word. Unless it was her idea. Somehow
he couldn't see that happening. She still thought of him as
her boss and nothing more. He could see it in her eyes,
hear it in her voice. How in the hell was he going to get
her to think of him as her husband?

Emily wished for nothing more than something to wear
to bed besides a silk negligee. But after dumping her suitcase out on the bed and going through her new clothes one
more time in hopes of coming across a pair of sweatpants
and a sweatshirt, she gave up. She'd been too preoccupied,
too busy to do her own packing, which she now regretted.
Peggy had thought she was going on a real honeymoon.

Now she realized she had no choice of sleepwear, given
her trousseau, so she chose an ivory satin coverup, repacked
her suitcase, grabbed an extra pillow and a blanket from
the closet and walked into the living room where Ben had
turned off the lights and started a fire in the fireplace.

"Oh," she said, pulling the satin robe tightly around her.

"I thought you were—I thought you'd want to go to bed. It's been a long day." She yawned again.

"Yes it has. Are you enjoying your honeymoon, Emily?" he asked.

She studied his face, lit only by the flickering flames, and wondered what he meant. Wondering if it was a trick question.

"Yes, of course."

There was a long silence. She leaned against the wall with her hands behind her, and he sat in one of the rustic wooden chairs and stared into the flames. Finally, because the silence was making her jumpy and she didn't want to lie down and curl up on the hearth with her blanket like a homeless, pathetic orphan while he was still sitting there, she spoke.

"Are you?"

"Am I what, enjoying my honeymoon? Yes, of course. It's not quite what I imagined, but what the hell."

"I didn't know you'd imagined a honeymoon at all," she said. "Since you never planned on getting married."

"Good point," he said. "But now that I am married, I find the honeymoon so far has been rather frustrating." He leaned forward in his chair, gripped the iron poker from the fireplace so tightly his knuckles turned white, and stirred the fire.

She swallowed hard. She didn't have to speak. No answer was required of her. Yet she couldn't hold her tongue. Her curiosity was building along with the tension in the room. "In what way?" she asked.

He dropped the poker on the floor. The loud bang made her heart leap. Then he stood and crossed the room in two large steps to face her. She could feel the heat from his body radiate in her direction. She could smell the salt water that clung to his skin and the fresh air from his clothes.

She could hear the crackle of the dry fir branches burning in the fireplace.

He looked down at her, his eyes smoldering with more heat than in a blazing fireplace.

"You want to know how it's been frustrating?" he demanded, resting his large hands on her shoulders and pinning her to the wall. "I'll show you how."

She knew it was going to happen and yet she didn't resist. He pulled her close, closer until his chest pressed against her breasts. His strong, muscled thighs pressed against her legs, and she was trapped. The heat that pooled in the center of her being was spreading like a wildfire throughout her body. Could she have doused the fire? Pushed him away? Of course. Did she? Of course not. Why should she? It was her honeymoon. The only honeymoon she'd ever have. He was her husband. The only husband she'd ever have. Not forever, not until death parted them, but for one year.

She sighed a ragged sigh of surrender, put her arms around his neck and gave in to temptation. Her fingers threaded through his dark hair. How many times in the past three years had her fingers itched to do that very thing? How many times had she dragged her gaze from his face so as not to give away her feelings? The sensations that hit her were stronger than any wave. And they threatened to swamp her more surely and more dangerously than the waters of the sound.

She told herself it was all right. It was all right to let herself go. Touch and taste and look. Just once, she told herself. She'd been good for so long. So terribly long. Hiding her feelings. Swallowing her pride. Making her face a mask. Her skin tingled. Her robe shifted and twisted until the silk of her camisole was her only protection. That and her willpower, which was fast slipping away.

A surge of pure sexual desire came out of nowhere and made her knees weak. If she hadn't been clinging to him like a vine around an oak tree, she'd be on the floor by now. She told herself not to give in. If she did, she'd pay for it later. There was only heartbreak ahead. Her inner voice told her he only wanted her for one night or one year at best. But she wasn't listening to her inner voice. She was listening to Ben tell her how beautiful she was. She didn't believe him but, oh, how she wanted to.

"Emily, what you do to me. Where have you been all these years?" His lips brushed her ear. "Where have I been that I didn't notice you?"

Where had she been? She'd been hiding behind her glasses and her efficient manner. Where had he been? She had the answer to that, too. He'd been consorting with every gorgeous woman in town. But now was not the time to remind him. Even if she wanted to she couldn't.

Because his lips came down on hers, hard and hungry. His kiss held all the pent-up passion he'd been holding in check. When she kissed him back her kiss held all the pent-up passion she'd been holding in check. For three long years. He pulled back to gaze at her with passion-darkened eyes.

"I never knew, never dreamed...all this time," Ben muttered. His voice was ragged. His voice sounded shell-shocked in his ears. His heart was beating as fast as hers. He wanted her. He wanted her more than he thought possible. He traced the seam of her soft lips with his tongue, and she didn't resist. Shyly she welcomed his tongue as he explored the dark recesses of her mouth. Shyly she joined him in the dance of passion.

He wondered if he was the first man in her life. He wanted to be the first man in her life. To teach her what it was all about. He'd be gentle. He'd be considerate. He'd go slow. He trailed kisses along the curve of her cheek to her throat. He slid her nightgown off her shoulders and watched as the satin pooled around her feet. She gasped and crossed her arms over her breasts.

He drew in a sharp breath, delighting in her modesty, wanting to see more of those small perfect breasts, her rounded belly and long legs. Yes, he'd seen her in the tub, but he'd never imagined she would feel this way, respond this way, like she'd been shut up in a convent all these years.

In a way she had been shut up. In his office. He groaned. All the time he'd wasted. Gently he lifted her arms from her breasts and pinned them to her sides with his hands. Then he lowered his head and reverently put his tongue to one rose-tipped breast. She gave a violent shudder and collapsed against him. With one arm around her gently rounded bottom, he scooped her up in his arms, all one-hundred-plus pounds of her, completely naked and completely his. His wife. The thought made him swell with pride. His body throbbed. He was on his way to consummate his marriage. Just a few brief steps down the hall.

It had all paid off. The call to the desk clerk, the change in accommodations. He and Emily. It was meant to be. At least for tonight. At least for his honeymoon. His promise of no sex was pushed to the back of his mind. His good intentions forgotten.

Until the phone rang.

Emily wriggled out of his arms, and he reluctantly set her back on her feet. She didn't even give him a chance to say, *Don't answer it. Let it ring. It can't be that important.* Nothing could be as important as making love to his wife. He could see her whole body tremble as she frantically groped for her nightgown on the floor.

Finally he picked up the phone.

"Yes?" he snapped.

It was Lipsett, the head of the oil company's overseas operations, calling from London. "Sorry to bother you, boss, I've had a hell of a time tracking you down. I hear you're on your honeymoon, but I thought you ought to know that there's trouble in the field."

"This had better be important. What is it?"

He leaned against the sofa and watched Emily pull her nightgown back on over her hips, feet first. Her hair was tangled, her face flushed, and it was all he could do to hold on to the receiver. He wanted to reach for her, to tell her he meant every word. That he wanted her more than he'd ever wanted anyone. But there was something about the set of her shoulders, the way she avoided his gaze that told him it was over. At least for tonight. Damn, damn, damn.

"Get on with it, man, I haven't got all night," Ben said.

He listened to Lipsett explain the situation and told him he'd get on it right away and get back to him. When he hung up, Emily was standing across the room, her arms crossed over her waist. As if nothing had ever happened between them. As if she was once again his assistant and they'd never left the office. Never changed roles, never gotten married.

"What is it?" she asked.

"There's been a blowout at the Makajar field, and the well is on fire."

"Was anyone hurt?"

"No, as soon as it blew, everyone left the rig. Before it caught fire."

"Thank heavens. So it's still burning?" she asked.

"Yes. We've got to get in touch with Jack Blake, the oil-well fire expert. I don't suppose you have his number."

"I have it in my file. I know exactly where it is, but that doesn't do us any good. He's not listed. There's no one at the office to find it for us until morning." She ran her hand through her hair, leaving it standing up like a halo around her head. "Wait a minute, I have an idea." Her idea was to call someone who could call someone who might know Jack's unlisted number. But it took hours and much persuasion on Ben's part. Those who knew the number were under strict orders not to give it out.

While Emily wrote down names and numbers, and Ben placed call after call, it was exactly like old times. Like being back in the office solving a problem. They worked well together, fed on each other's ideas. They always had. Always would. Her quiet assurance calmed his nerves. His suggestions stimulated her imagination. He felt a surge of confidence. Together they could do anything. Solve any problem.

Maybe it was wrong to want more from their relationship. Maybe he was pushing too hard for something that wasn't meant to be. While waiting for a callback, Ben paced back and forth, picturing the flames spreading, fearful of loss of property, revenues and general destruction. When they finally reached the firefighter he promised to be on his way with a team in twenty-four hours. Ben called Lipsett back and heaved a sigh of relief. He ran his hand through his hair and sat down to face the dying embers in the fireplace.

"I almost didn't answer that call," he told Emily.

"It's a good thing you did."

"Lipsett said to send along his best wishes."

She looked blank. She also looked tired.

"On your recent marriage."

"Oh, that."

He was disappointed that she could dismiss it so readily. Of course she'd only married him because he'd pressured her, bribed her, so what did he expect?

"Go to bed, Emily, you're exhausted."

"Not any more than you are," she said.

He stood. "I mean it. Either you go on your own or I'll carry you down the hall and I'll put you in bed myself."

Emily stood, knowing by the gruff tone of his voice that he meant every word. Part of her was longing to call his bluff, wanting nothing more than to have him carry her down the hall and put her to bed. If this were a real marriage, he'd go with her. They'd tumble into bed together, make love all night under the soft cotton sheets and fall asleep at dawn the way honeymooners are supposed to do. If it hadn't been for the phone...

"But you said we'd take turns," she said, buying time. Time to think about what to do.

"You said that. I never agreed to that. What kind of man would let his wife sleep in a chair on their honeymoon?"

"A nineties man. A man who believes in the equality of the sexes."

He snorted. "If that's your definition of a nineties man, then I'm glad I'm not one. And I don't think you want one." He walked across the room and braced his hands against the wall, trapping her with his arms, but giving her plenty of space. This time she was prepared. She was not going to let him reduce her knees to jelly, turn her body temperature up above the point of combustion.

"What do you want, Emily? What kind of man are you looking for?" His voice was tight with fatigue and something else. Something dangerously like suppressed passion.

She stiffened her spine. This time she would not fall apart in his arms. He would not seduce her. She was happy the phone had rung. Grateful for the interruption. Because if it hadn't, she was afraid she would have given in. She knew she would have given in. And now, right now, her virginity that weighed so heavily on her like an albatross around her neck would be a thing of the past. She'd be married in every sense of the word except for the forever part.

"I'm not looking," she said. "You're the one who was looking, not me. So you tell me, Ben, what is it you want in a woman?" This was her new tack. Keep on the offensive. Keep him answering the questions, not her.

"Do you want to know, Emily?" he asked, his rugged face in shadows now as the fire went out completely. "Do you really want to know?"

She nodded.

"I want someone soft and sweet on the outside but strong on the inside. Someone who can take and give. Take and give criticism, help, and most of all to give and take love." His voice dropped, his gaze held hers for a long moment. She wanted to remind him he didn't believe in love. But she didn't. She wanted to believe she was the kind of woman he was looking for. She wanted to believe it so badly she ached.

"For how long, Ben?" she murmured. "For how long?"

He didn't answer. He didn't have to. She knew the answer. For a night or a week or a year at the very most. Then he wanted his freedom, his precious freedom.

He picked her up and carried her to the bedroom. But it was different this time. For one thing, the phone didn't ring. And for another he had no intention of staying. She could tell by the way he held her. Out in front of him like a sack of potatoes. As if he could hardly wait to get rid of her. He set her in the middle of the bed and left her there. Without another word. She heard his footsteps go back down the short hall. Exhausted, she lay in the huge soft bed. Too tired to worry about him. Too tired to worry about anything. But his words lingered in her subconscious. Soft

on the outside, strong on the inside. She must be strong.
Mustn't let him get through to her. Strong.

He was dressed when she staggered out of the bedroom
the next morning. Blinding sunlight shone through the huge
picture window. Puget Sound sparkled in the distance like
her diamond ring.

"Let's go," he said.

She looked blank. "What about the fire?"

"It's under control. It's not out, but they've got a handle
on it."

She rubbed her eyes. "You should have wakened me.
How long have you been up?"

"An hour. Get your clothes on. The boat leaves at ten."

Only last night he was taking her clothes off. Now he
was ordering her to put them on. Briskly. Today he was
the old Ben she'd left behind in San Francisco. He was all
business. She was relieved. Happy. Only a slight pang of
disappointment was left. Nothing to worry about.

She got dressed in another new outfit. Straight-legged
cotton hopsack pants in butter-yellow, with a matching
sweater she threw around her shoulders. After all these
years she finally realized how her siblings felt when they
put on a costume and became a different character. She,
too, was getting paid to play a part. Maybe she'd inherited
some of the Claybourne dramatic skills after all. After all,
she'd fooled a whole churchful of people into thinking that
she was a real bride.

She wondered if actors were ever afraid they'd grow too
attached to their roles and forget who they really were.
When she walked outside to the deck where Ben was waiting he told her he'd arranged for them to go to Vancouver
Island by ferry to visit the Butchart Gardens.

Her eyes widened with delight. Her mouth fell open with
surprise.

"Have you heard of them?" he asked.

"Of course. Their rose garden is famous. And the sunken garden they made from an old quarry. I've always wanted to go there. I didn't know it was close enough— Oh, Ben, are you sure you won't be bored? I mean it's just a lot of flowers and—"

"I like flowers," he assured her. "And I like seeing you look at flowers."

Once aboard the ferry, they sailed past summer houses on bluffs, dense-forested islands and wild stretches of coastline toward Friday Harbor where they'd catch the Canadian ferry to Vancouver. The wind blew her hair across her cheek and dislodged the sweater from one shoulder. He tucked her hair behind her ear and tied the sweater over her chest. A tremor of awareness skittered through her body. He gave her a brief smile then turned his attention to the passing scenery.

Yes, he'd obviously decided last night was a mistake. It took just one phone call from the office and it reminded him of who he was and where his priorities lay. She too quickly turned her attention to the small islands with sandy shorelines. The sun warmed her skin and she breathed in the salt air and inhaled the scent of pine trees.

She'd chosen the right place for a honeymoon. It was too bad she hadn't chosen the right groom. One who was in love with the bride. But she hadn't really had a choice. It was Ben or no one. But you couldn't have everything, she reminded herself. And she had quite a bit. She had a wonderful day to look forward to. A visit to a famous garden. And the company of the man she loved. Never mind that he didn't love her. Love wasn't all it was cracked up to be. It could be downright painful. No, she couldn't ask for more. Wishing he'd love her back was a waste of time. It wasn't going to happen.

Chapter Seven

It was true. Ben liked watching Emily admire the flowers. When her face lit up at the sight of the rose garden and its thousands of blooms, she was as lovely as a rose in bloom herself. Like one of those stunning pale pink hybrids she was looking at. He wondered how he'd ever thought she was plain. Actually he never thought about how she looked at all. He'd always admired her intelligence. Her good taste and her good sense. But now there was something else. He didn't know what to call it. It wasn't just the way she looked. It was an awareness, a sense of who she was and what she was becoming. He'd seen it in her eyes last night. He wanted to see it again. Wanted to tell her again how beautiful she was.

But he wasn't going to.

While they strolled the gardens, Ben and Emily learned how Jenny Butchart made a garden out of a limestone quarry her industrialist husband had purchased for his business. She'd turned a bleak, empty pit into a sunken garden by taking tons of topsoil from nearby farms. And what a garden. Besides the rose garden, which replaced the kitchen vegetable patch, there was the Japanese garden on the sea side of the house, and a sumptuous symmetrical Italian garden on the site of their former tennis court.

When they paused for afternoon tea on the porch of the old-fashioned restaurant, Emily read aloud from the brochure how Mr. Butchart had taken great pride in his wife's work. How he shared her passion for flowers and he himself collected ornamental birds, which frolicked among her beautiful blooms. Peacocks once strolled on the front lawn, and trained pigeons made their home on the site of the begonia bower. A parrot lived in the main house. Ben studied the rapt expression on Emily's face as she set the brochure down and gazed off at the vista of ornamental shrubs and vast lawns.

"Envious?" Ben asked.

"A little," she admitted.

"I can't compete with Mr. Butchart, but I do have a terrace, you know. A fairly large empty terrace."

"But..."

"Yes, I know. You once suggested I have a garden there, but I didn't want the responsibility of taking care of it. But now that you're going to be living there..."

"Only temporarily," she reminded him.

"You can plant in pots. Then you can take everything with you when you leave."

He thought she'd be pleased. After all, it had been her idea to turn his terrace into a garden when he'd moved in there a year and a half ago. Now he couldn't tell what she thought. She picked up her teacup, then she set it down. Her lower lip trembled.

"What is it? What did I say?" he asked. "I thought you'd be happy."

"I am. Of course I am. I'd love to make a garden on

your terrace. Maybe you'll get so attached to it you won't want me to take it away.''

He shook his head. ''A garden would be wasted on me. I'm never there. It's just a place to hang my hat, so to speak. I want to be free to come and go. As you know, I spend a great deal of time working, whether at the office or out of town. And when I'm in town…''

''You're *on* the town,'' Emily said.

''That's right. At least I was. Don't think I'll be out carousing while we're married. I intend to be a faithful husband, Emily. For as long as we're married.'' He covered her hand with his. ''Just so you know.''

She nodded, but he couldn't tell what she was thinking. She seemed to be more interested in the scones and the clotted cream on the tea tray. It seemed that either she didn't care if he was a faithful husband, or she didn't believe him. He wanted her to care, and he wanted her to believe him. But he didn't know what else to say. It was safer to talk about flowers. So after they finished their tea, they continued their discussion of the terrace garden, as she advised him what flowers would do well in the foggy San Francisco microclimate on top of his building.

When they finished their tour, they hopped aboard the ferry, and before returning to the hotel they dined on steamed clams at a small restaurant on the dock of Orcas Island.

When they arrived back at the fifty-four-room villa that served as the main building of their resort, Ben went to check with the concierge about going whale watching the next day, and Emily strolled to the front desk to ask if they had any messages. The clerk said no, then asked her if the accommodations were all right.

''I had reserved a two-bedroom cottage,'' she said. ''I don't know what went wrong, but…''

"But your husband changed the order," the clerk said, after consulting his reservation book.

"What?"

"Yes, he called yesterday, and we were happy to oblige when we heard it was your honeymoon."

Emily gripped the edge of the counter. "He told you that?" she asked.

"Oh, yes. Congratulations, by the way."

"Thank you." Emily's thoughts were thrown into turmoil. How could he do that? Why did he say that?

As they walked back to their cottage along a path lit with gas lanterns, Ben described the whale-watching tour he'd booked them on for the next day. But Emily scarcely heard him.

She walked straight into the bedroom, though she didn't want to even go near it. She was determined to let him sleep there that night, but she needed her things. While riffling through her suitcase for her cosmetic bag, she noted that the maids had turned down the bed and left fresh chocolate chip cookies on the bedside stand. In spite of her good intentions she let out a wistful sigh. If this were a real marriage, they'd be in bed now, feeding each other cookies, licking the chocolate off each other's lips....

Deliberately she grabbed her nightgown, blanket and cosmetic bag, and with her arms full she turned and bumped into Ben.

"Let's have no more nonsense about where you're going to sleep," he said, steadying her with his hands on her arms.

"Ben, we agreed—"

"I never agreed," he said.

"We wouldn't have this problem if—"

"If you'd be reasonable, Emily. This bed is plenty big enough for two."

"Is that what you think? You think we ought to sleep together?" she asked incredulously. "Is that why you changed the reservation? Is that why you asked for a one-bedroom instead of two?" She was so angry she felt like her eyes must be shooting sparks.

But instead of denying it or even looking embarrassed, Ben said, "What's wrong with that? We *are* married, you know."

"It's not real."

"Let's make it real." His meaning was clear. His eyes were dark with passion. She couldn't move, couldn't breathe. She dropped the blanket, the nightgown and the cosmetic case at her feet. Shivers went up and down her spine.

"You don't mean that," she said weakly, knowing full well he did mean it.

"Tell me you don't want to make love with me, Emily," he murmured, as he caught her chin with his hand and forced her to meet his dark gaze. "Tell me you don't want to spend the night with me in that bed there. Say you don't want me to kiss you here—" he ran his hand down from her chin down to the hollow between her breasts "—and here…" He let his thumbs make concentric circles around her breasts, closing in on her nipples until they beaded and peaked under his touch.

All the breath whooshed out of her lungs and left her speechless. If she could have spoken she would have begged him to stop this exquisite torture. She would have said no to his questions. No, no and no. But she couldn't speak. She was trembling all over her body, from head to toe. She'd never wanted anything as much as she wanted Ben to make love to her. To kiss her there and there and there.

But she knew what would happen if he did. He'd find

out she was a novice. She wouldn't be able to hide her inexperience from his all-knowing gaze. And even if she did, where would their lovemaking lead? In a matter of days they'd be back to San Francisco where, even though they were living under one roof, they'd slip back into their roles as boss and employee.

She wavered. On the other hand, she'd at least have a honeymoon to remember. Out of the corner of her eye she saw the bed turned down, a glimpse of soft white sheets and plumped-up pillows. She felt herself weaken. It would be so easy to say yes. So easy to slip off her clothes and leave them on the floor. So easy to watch him undress, to see him in all his naked glory. To let him teach her everything she didn't know, about the physical side of love. If only he loved her. If only he wanted to be married for more than a year. If only...

"No." It was the hardest decision she'd ever made. The most difficult word she'd ever spoken. She wrenched herself away from him, turned on her heels and fled the bedroom where temptation hung in the air like a thousand fragrant polyantha roses.

After she showered, she took her blanket and went to the living room. She tried not to listen as he turned on the shower, but she heard the water run for a long, long time before he walked back to the bedroom. She watched the lights go off and listened to the silence in the cottage. He was probably sleeping soundly in that big bed while she huddled in her blanket on the floor in front of the stone-cold fireplace.

And whose fault was that? It was hers. This whole thing was her fault. She never should have married him. She'd been perfectly happy as his assistant. Loving him from afar. So safe, so secure, so much in the background, so comfortable. Now every day was a challenge. A challenge she wasn't up to.

She got up and tried to sleep in the chair. It was no use. Her whole body tingled, especially the sensitive spots where he'd touched her. She turned on the lamp and plucked an illustrated book on Washington State birds from the bookshelf. It was so boring she finally fell asleep before she'd turned the second page.

That's where Ben found her in the early morning, ensconced in a chair, the lamp spilling light on her soft brown hair, her chin tucked into her chest, her book on the floor. His heart ached for her. So stubborn, so obstinate, so headstrong, so…so damned sweet and so desirable that he wanted her more than he'd ever wanted any woman before. He didn't know why. She wasn't his type. She wasn't really beautiful. She wasn't strictly speaking sexy, either, not in the obvious way a lot of other women were.

He sighed loudly, picked her up and carried her into the bedroom. She murmured something and snuggled into his arms. She was so warm, so soft, that he had to grit his teeth and clench his jaw to keep from getting into bed with her. Instead he lay her under the covers in the spot he'd just vacated, and with only one backward glance, he changed into shorts and a T-shirt and went out running. The only honeymooner in history, he imagined, to have to run off his frustrations. The others were all in bed making love to their wives. He'd tried. God knows he'd tried everything. Well, almost everything.

When he got back she was dressed, this time in stretch pants that hugged her long legs, a T-shirt and a thick sweater tied around her waist. All those years together and he never noticed her delectable body. All those wasted years he'd spent lusting after women who had many attributes, but with whom he had nothing in common, when Emily was right there in his office.

On the other hand, what would she have done if he'd suddenly come on to her, asked her out on dates and tried to kiss her in the boardroom? He'd have had no better luck than he was having now. She wanted nothing to do with him, except in an official capacity. Every time he tried to cross the line, she withdrew.

Neither spoke of what had happened the night before. Neither spoke at all. What was there to say? Ben stood in the doorway looking at her, giving her a long, leisurely look that made Emily's stomach churn with anxiety. Was he going to start in again? Would she have the strength to say no again or would she give in? She wanted to know how she'd gotten into the bed and how long she'd been there, but she wasn't going to ask.

She couldn't tear her eyes from his muscled thighs, his T-shirt damp with sweat or his hair slicked back from his face by the wind. When his eyes met hers she couldn't catch her breath. As if she'd been running instead of him. They stood there while the silence stretched like a taut rubber band and her questions hung in the air waiting to be asked.

"How did I get into that bed?" she asked.

"I put you there."

"Oh. Then I overslept. Why didn't you wake me?" she asked at last.

"You looked so peaceful, I couldn't. Besides…"

"Did you say we were going whale watching?" she asked, afraid he'd say something about last night.

"Among other things. I've asked the hotel for a picnic lunch so we can be out all day. I'd like to climb Mt. Constitution too if you're up to it."

"Of course. Whatever you want to do," she said politely.

"It's your honeymoon, too," he said pointedly.

And what a honeymoon, she thought. Only five days to go. Would she get through them without losing her head, her heart and her virginity? Did she want to?

Emily got through the day. And the next day and the day after that. It was the nights that tested her resolve. Her determination to keep her wits, her calm and her virginity were tested night after night. Ben insisted she take the bed, and on that point she gave in. But on every other issue she stood firm. No matter how often she felt his hot-and-heavy glances follow her as she walked down that hall to the bedroom, how many excuses he made to come into the bedroom, lingering, sitting on the edge of the bed, talking…. She pretended not to notice that their relationship had changed. But she noticed, oh, how she noticed.

He was after something. She just didn't know what. She suspected it was just sex. But she wasn't sexy. She didn't understand. How did he feel about her? Grateful? Kindly? Sympathetic? Curious? Or something else? How long had he felt that way? What was he going to do about it? Nothing, she hoped.

On their last night, the night before they were to go back to San Francisco, she was congratulating herself on getting through the week without making a fool of herself. As far as she knew he had no idea how she felt about him. And that's the way it had to be. If he knew, he'd feel sorry for her. If he knew, he might make love to her out of some misguided sense of charity.

That night she ran into him coming out of the bathroom. Literally. He was coming out, smelling like his European shampoo, wearing only a towel, one hand carrying his shaving kit, the other gripping the edge of the towel. She was on her way back from the tiny kitchen in her nightgown with a glass of juice in her hand.

As they collided, she dropped her glass, juice spattered and he dropped his towel. She reached for the glass, he reached for the towel. Amusement flickered in his dark eyes. A hot flush suffused her whole body as she tried in vain to keep her eyes averted from his potent masculinity.

"I'm sorry, Emily," he said, carefully rewrapping his towel around his waist.

She managed a nonchalant shrug of her shoulders and repeated what he'd once said to her on the first day of their honeymoon. "Don't worry. I didn't see anything I've never seen before." She hoped she gave the impression she'd seen lots of men in various stages of undress. Just as Ben had seen many women. It was too bad she couldn't keep her voice steady, it undermined her credibility.

"Really?" he said, blocking her way so she couldn't escape to the bedroom. "How do I measure up?"

Emily bit her lip. He was teasing her. She heard it in his voice, saw it in the curve of his lips. Hot tears of frustration pricked at her eyelids. What did he expect her to say?

"What is it? What did I say to make you cry?" he asked, his forehead creased in an anxious frown.

"N-nothing. I'm just on edge tonight. Thinking about all the work that's piled up in our absence." There, that was a logical excuse for panicking.

"If you won't tell me how I measure up, then tell me how this trip has measured up to the other vacations you've taken," he said.

She braced her hand against the wall. "It's been lovely. The scenery, the food, the activities have all been superb."

"And the company?" he asked, his head tilted inquiringly to one side.

"Of course the company was superb, too."

"What else could you say?" he mused. "Since I'm your boss. Tell me, will you be sorry to leave here tomorrow?"

Sorry? Sorry to get back to real life, to a bedroom, a bathroom and a dressing room of her own, a huge condo where she wasn't likely to bump into him at every turn? Where he wouldn't carry her to bed and accidentally brush against her at every turn? Or burst into the bathroom on some flimsy excuse? Go back to work where he was her boss and not her husband? "Not really," she said casually. "Will you?"

"Yes, in a way. I hate to leave here without doing everything I set out to do."

"But you climbed Mt. Constitution, we saw a whale breach off the dock, we watched seals sunning themselves on the rocks, we've eaten clams and oysters and salmon, you've been sailing and...and... What more could you want?" As soon as the words left her mouth, she knew she shouldn't have said them.

"What do you think I want, Emily?" If his words didn't convey his meaning, the look he gave her, a look heavy with intent, a look laden with white-hot desire did. She should have known better than to ask a loaded question like that. Especially when she had no way to escape. He was blocking her way to the bedroom. He leaned forward and paused, his lips only inches from her mouth. She could almost feel his lips come down on hers, almost taste the after-dinner coffee on his breath, almost feel his tongue probe the secret recesses of her mouth, seeking her participation in a duel of love.

She couldn't move, she couldn't speak. She was waiting, longing, yearning for his kiss. A kiss that would tell her more than words how he felt about her. But when it came she was not prepared. Not ready for the fierce intensity, not prepared to be possessed like that, with only his lips. She was only dimly aware that he'd dropped his shaving kit and then his towel to set his hands free. Free to run his hands down her back, to cup her bottom and draw her close, so close she felt the surge of his bare masculinity against her belly.

There was only the pale sheer silk of her nightgown between them. Only one layer of fabric between her and her husband. Husband in name only. So far. If that layer was gone they'd have crossed another barrier, and she would have no more defenses left. She'd be lost forever, and her love would be a secret no longer. If they began their married life this way, there'd be no turning back. And by the end of the year she'd be unable to walk away from him. Unless she wanted that to happen, she had to take the first step now. Walk away now. Now before it was too late.

Since she couldn't walk forward, she backed out of his embrace and willed herself to keep walking. One step at a time, until he stopped following her. Until he stood in the hallway watching her go, an unfathomable expression on his face.

"Good night, Emily," he said, an underlying hint of sadness in his voice. Or was it merely disappointment, or perhaps just a bruised ego?

She closed the door after her, unable to even say goodnight to him.

When they returned to San Francisco the next day, Ben found to his surprise and dismay that his family was still there, ensconced in his apartment. He'd wanted to share this homecoming with Emily. And Emily alone. It was important that she consider it her home, too. But there they were. His big, happy, noisy family. Their music and laughter, as well as the smell of exotic spices wafted down the hallway to greet them before they even got to the door. Before Ben could take his key from his pocket, his father threw the door open and hugged both him and Emily, kissing them on both cheeks.

The old sheik explained that they'd meant to leave the day before, but their chartered plane was delayed, and so there they were. Spread out all over the place, aunts, uncles, nieces, nephews. They hoped the newlyweds wouldn't mind.

Ben noted Emily's forced smile and heard her assure them she didn't. He also noted that her smile faded as soon as she noticed her room had been commandeered by his three cousins. There was nothing he could do. No way he could explain that he wasn't sleeping with his bride. Or his father would know he hadn't fulfilled his end of the bargain.

He would say this for his bride: she was putting up a brave front. But he knew she didn't want to sleep with him; she'd made that abundantly clear. His father had already taken her bag and put it next to Ben's in his wood-paneled bedroom.

Emily couldn't be angry. She only felt a huge wave of fatigue sweep over her. The fatigue that comes from pretending day after day. She'd thought that when they got to the apartment she would finally be able to relax and stop acting the part of the happy bride, but she couldn't. Not when his family was so warm and kind and so undeniably happy to see them. His mother was in the kitchen roasting a lamb, stuffing grape leaves and making halvah candy. Restless, Emily wandered from room to room, but there was nowhere to hide. In the kitchen she offered to help his mother but she waved her away.

Dinner was a noisy affair, twelve people clustered around the polished maple dining room table. The conversation was half in Arabic and half in English for Emily's benefit, with everyone making a special effort to make her feel a part of the family. Which made her feel worse than ever. What would they say when they got their divorce? Would they blame her? She tried to eat but there was a lump in her throat. They coaxed her, they begged her to taste a little of this, a little of that, but that just made it worse.

Finally she excused herself and almost ran from the room. She hoped they didn't think her rude. She hoped Ben might explain better than she could that she was tired. She imagined that when Ben finally joined her in his bedroom their smiles would broaden and his mother and father would exchange knowing looks. Naturally they'd assume their son and his new wife were making love behind the closed doors. That's what everyone assumed. The maid at the hotel, the bellboy, the clerk and God knew who else.

She was standing at the window watching the fog rush in through the Golden Gate when Ben finally came in and closed the door behind him.

"I'm sorry about this," Ben said. "I had no idea they'd still be here. If I could I'd sleep on the couch, but..."

"You can't. Your parents would wonder. I can see your finding a wife has meant a lot to them. I'm just sorry—" Sorry it wasn't a real marriage. Sorry he hadn't found someone more suitable, someone he could love. Someone he could stay married to, have children with and live happily every after.

"Yes?" he asked.

"Never mind. Anyway, it's just for one night."

"Yes, they'll be gone tomorrow. If I have to put them all up at the Ritz Carlton, they'll be gone," he muttered.

"It's all right," Emily assured him, sitting on the edge of her bed and kicking off her shoes. "Your bed is big enough for both of us, I mean we won't get in each other's way,'' she said, carefully avoiding his gaze. It was time she got over her fear of sleeping with Ben. He was too much of a gentleman to ever do anything she didn't want him to do. If she were honest with herself she'd admit she was more afraid of her own reactions than his. ''It's ridiculous for one of us to sleep on a chair or on the floor.''

Ben's silence either meant he was stunned by her change in attitude, or he didn't care one way or the other. On the way home they'd both been quiet, lost in thought, perhaps having regrets, anticipating their new life. She was afraid Ben was angry with her for running away from him on their last night. He probably didn't understand what made her take one step forward and two steps backward in their relationship. She barely understood herself.

All she knew was that she was tired of keeping him at a distance. For one week she'd fought off his advances and fought off her own inner feelings. She was tired, so tired of fighting. She just wanted to crawl between the sheets and put her head on the pillow and sleep for about a week. She couldn't force another smile or answer another question from a well-meaning relative.

When she came out of Ben's well-appointed bathroom, which smelled of his shaving cream, he was already in bed, with the sheet resting halfway up his chest. She prayed that he was already asleep. Despite her best intentions she wondered what he was wearing. She could see his chest was bare. But what else? The dark hair that lightly covered his chest reminded her how it felt to her fingers. Soft and springy and...

Quickly she turned off the light, got in on the far side of the bed and closed her eyes. Outside their door she could hear soft footsteps and muted voices speaking low. She knew what they were thinking. She knew what they were saying, too, even though it was in another language:

Didn't she look tired? Do you suppose she's pregnant already?

Shhh, they'll hear you.

She's so different from all his other women.

Ahmed, what if he doesn't love her?

He will, Farida, he will.

No, he won't, she thought as a tear trickled down her cheek. And then another. No, he won't.

"Emily." Ben's voice was as dark and deep as the night outside the window. "Are you crying?"

Chapter Eight

"No," she said, and burst into tears. All the pent-up frustrations of the past week erupted as she buried her face in her pillow.

He sat up in bed. "What's wrong?" he asked.

"Nothing," she gasped between the sobs that grew louder the more she tried to muffle them.

Instead of sliding across the bed, he got up, walked around to her side, sat on the edge of the bed and turned her gently toward him. "Don't tell me 'Nothing' when you're obviously upset about something."

She squeezed her eyes shut, but she knew exactly how he looked. He had a frown on his face. He hated being lied to. And she was lying to him.

She sat up and stared straight ahead, careful to avoid looking at his face or at his bare chest or at whatever he was or wasn't wearing to bed. She opened her mouth to explain she was perfectly all right, just a little overwrought, but the tears kept coming. She *never* cried. She wasn't the weepy, emotional type. Then why... Why now?

He put his hands on her shoulders and very slowly turned her to face him. Then he wiped a tear from her cheek with the pad of his thumb. Her heart hammered so loudly his whole family could have heard it.

"Don't cry, Emily," he said, his voice so low she almost didn't hear him. "Please don't cry. It's my family, isn't it? They can be overwhelming at times. But tomorrow they'll be gone and we'll be alone. Just us. Back to normal."

He ran his finger along the outline of her cheek. She shuddered. She couldn't explain that it wasn't his family that made her cry. She couldn't speak at all. His touch was too gentle. Too kind. With that one gesture he destroyed the last of her defenses against him. She drew a long, shaky breath and collapsed against his bare chest. She felt his heart pound in time to hers. He lifted her chin and forced her to look at him.

She couldn't say anything. She couldn't look away. His eyes were so deep she felt she was drowning in his gaze. Foolish girl, she looked for love. But she found only passion and a hint of anxiety. In that brief moment she sensed he was as unsure of her as she was of him. It gave her a feeling of power. A rush of pure sexual excitement surged through her body. He kissed her eyelids, he paused and then kissed the corners of her mouth. He was seducing her. She was being seduced for the first time in her life. The knowledge filled her with a burning desire that spread to every pore of her body.

He didn't love her, but he wanted her. For now that would do, she decided finally. She had enough love for both of them. He had enough experience. Should she tell him she had none or would he find out soon enough?

With one hand he slid the thin strap of her plum silk teddy over her shoulder and brushed her tender bare breasts with his broad fingers. She moaned softly in the back of her throat and instinctively reached for the waistband of his silk boxer shorts. He groaned and pulled her up out of the bed with him.

"Go ahead," he said gruffly. "Take them off. Do it."

She did it. Shyly she tugged at his shorts and they came off. Now there was nothing between them. The sight of his beautiful body and his throbbing manhood made her weak. He lifted her up in his arms, and she wrapped her bare legs around his waist. He inhaled sharply, and somehow they landed in bed together, rolling over until they lay facing each other, side to side. He held her just far enough away to take a lazy tour of her body with his heated gaze, leaving her skin tingling. Then came his hands, his broad fingers lingering on the curve of her stomach, then moving slowly, sensuously to the juncture of her inner thigh.

The sensations were coming fast and furiously. She was losing control. She was scared, the kind of scared you feel on the top of the roller coaster just before the descent. "Ben, no…"

"Do you want me to stop?"

"No…no." What, and deprive her of the steepest, fastest, most exciting ride of her life?

He didn't stop, his hands continued their journey, stroking, caressing, down the length of her legs until he stopped at her toes. There his lips took over, drawing each toe into his mouth and sucking until she thought she'd explode.

"Hold on, Emily, hold on, my darling. I'm not finished yet," he murmured, kissing his way up her legs, past the silver anklet. The anklet that meant she belonged to him.

She didn't know what to expect. No idea what was coming next. She just knew the tension was building, building with every kiss until it was unbearable. Soon she would not be able to hold on. Not for another moment. When his lips reached her core her heart flew to her throat and her world splintered into a thousand pieces. She wanted to shout, she wanted to scream, she wanted to cry out his name, but somewhere in her subconscious she knew they weren't alone. So she clamped her hand over her mouth and cried. Great gulping sobs.

She who never cried had cried twice tonight. Each time for different reasons. This time he braced his hands on to her shoulders and kissed her tears away.

"Shhh, don't cry," he said.

"But Ben...I didn't know."

He nodded. He knew. He must have known it was her first time. She wondered if she'd made a fool of herself. Before she could worry about her inexperience he took her hand and placed it against his manhood.

She gasped at the size and strength of it, surprised at the velvet touch of something so powerful. Shyly, curiously, she ran her fingers up and over the shaft.

He hissed his approval. "Yes," he said. "Yes, Emily, yes."

She arched herself to give him access to her most sensitive, most vulnerable self. Slowly, carefully, she guided him in until he filled her so completely, so perfectly she marveled at the miracle of it. Slowly, carefully, so as not to hurt her, he began his rhythmic thrusts. The little sounds she made in the back of her throat goaded him on. Faster and faster until she climaxed again and again. She gripped his shoulders, unaware of the marks she was making on his skin or of the jumble of words that burst from her lips. Words of passion and of desire.

When he shattered inside of her, he called her name. Afraid someone would hear him she covered his mouth with her hand and he kissed her palm. It was the sweetest, tenderest of kisses. She had to press her lips together to keep from blurting that she loved him. It would have sent him fleeing—out to the couch, despite his family, or at least to the floor.

Instead they lay together in the middle of that huge bed, her bare bottom pressed against his thighs, his arms around her, his hands splayed across her breasts. Her heart was full to overflowing. She never knew it would be like that. The give and take, the mystical merging of two beings into one through a physical act.

When he stirred, he muttered something she could barely hear.

"I forgot," he mumbled. "Damn, you should have reminded me. Forgot to use protection." He exhaled loudly, then pressed his lips to the back of her neck. And promptly fell asleep. Leaving Emily jarred into the realization that if it was a real marriage, protection would not be an issue. At his age, and at hers, they'd be trying to get pregnant to add to the family tree.

Their baby would have his dark eyes, and hair the color of midnight. She'd quit her job and stay at home. But not here. They'd have a house with a rose garden in the suburbs. She squeezed her eyes shut to block the baby image, to get rid of the baby thoughts. Ben didn't even want a wife or a garden, let alone a baby. No, the most she could hope for was that he'd still want her for his assistant.

But would she want to be his assistant when the year was up? Back to making dates for him, ordering flowers for his girlfriends? No. She would leave. Walk out of his life completely and start another one. She'd done it before. She'd left home and come to San Francisco. They'd begged her not to go, told her they needed her, that she'd never make it on her own. But she had. And she could do it again. Relieved after coming to that decision, pushing her questions, her worries and a nagging feeling of regret to the back of her mind, Emily finally slept.

* * *

When Ben awoke, she was gone. Somehow he knew she'd be gone. But that didn't ease the ache. Though she was only gone as far as the shower, she wasn't there in his bed where he wanted her. He wanted her with a fierce longing that startled him. He told himself it was because she was his wife. But deep down he knew it was because she was Emily.

The surprising part was not that she'd fled, but that she'd made love with him at all. He'd suspected she was a virgin. He'd suspected there were no other men in her life. For that he was immensely grateful. For once in his life he didn't know how to proceed with a woman. He, who was always in control, had lost it.

He was even more confused when she walked briskly into the bedroom from the bathroom, completely dressed in a pair of khaki slacks and a pullover shirt. She waltzed through the room with a breezy good-morning while he sat on the edge of the bed wondering what in the hell was going on. While he'd enjoyed the most incredible love-making of his life, she acted like it was just another roll in the hay.

As she reached for the doorknob, he leaped up, despite his total state of undress, and grabbed her by the arm. "Where in the hell are you going?" he demanded.

Her eyes widened. "Shhh, they'll hear you."

"I don't give a damn if the whole world hears me. I asked you a question."

Her lower lip trembled, and he could have kicked himself for getting angry. But damn it, he was frustrated, he was bewildered and he was still reeling from the most incredible night of his life.

"I'm going to eat breakfast," she said, her chin at that stubborn angle he recognized only too well.

"What's wrong?" he asked. "Are you angry because I went back on my word, is that it?"

"Yes."

"You could have stopped me. You could have said no. You didn't."

"I know. I'm not blaming you, I'm blaming myself."

"For what?" he demanded. "Making love with your husband?"

"You're not my husband," she said in a loud whisper. "Only on paper. You know it and I know it."

"Are you sorry for what happened?" he asked. He couldn't believe it had meant nothing to her.

"Yes," she said. But her face reddened and she averted her gaze. He didn't believe her.

"It was your first time," he said, running his thumb from her cheek to her throat. "I should have been more gentle."

"That's not it," she said. Then she wrenched her arm from his grasp and left the room.

He stood staring at the closed door for a long moment, wishing he knew how to handle her. This woman who was so different from all his other women.

It wasn't until late that afternoon when his family had finally left for the airport that he had a chance to talk to her. Not that she wanted to talk to him. That was clear. She'd been avoiding him, avoiding looking at him or talking to him whenever possible. While all day long she'd been friendly and gracious to his family.

The contrast between her attitude toward his family and toward him had him on the brink of a black hole of depression. He could tell they liked her—no they loved her. He could tell by the way they beamed their approval. He could tell by the knowing looks exchanged between his mother and father. And though Ben swore they weren't in love, his parents knew it was just a matter of time. As far as they were concerned he'd made the perfect choice.

Last night he would have agreed that he'd made the perfect choice. But not that he'd ever fall in love with her, since he still believed love was just a concept. Today he didn't know what to think. He wasn't sure what the protocol was for entering your wife's room, so he knocked on the door.

"Can we talk?" he asked, when she opened the door.

She peered at him over her glasses as if he was an aphid she'd just discovered in her rosebushes before she spoke. "Of course."

He stepped over a large cardboard box and walked over to the dresser, picked up her tortoiseshell brush and set it back down again. Then he looked in the walk-in closet, relieved to notice her old clothes were hanging there. The faint scent of roses wafted through the air. At least she wasn't so upset she was walking out on him. Instead she appeared to be settling in. Some of the black cloud of despair that was hanging over his head dissipated.

He turned around. She appeared to be utterly absorbed in taking books out of the cardboard box and putting them on a shelf. Just as if he wasn't there.

"Emily, put those books down and talk to me."

Obediently she dropped the books on the floor with a loud bang and sat in the large leather desk chair. He could have sworn they'd skipped the past three weeks and were back to their old roles of boss and assistant. At least, that was the way she was acting.

"About last night," he began.

"Let's forget about it, shall we?" she asked coolly.

"Is that what you want to do?" he asked.

"It's what we have to do. You're the one who said there would be no sex, you know."

"I know, I know. But you seemed..."

"Willing? I was. I admit that. That doesn't make it right."

"When I said that about no sex," Ben said, "I didn't know..."

"How convenient it would be to have a wife around?" Her voice was tinged with bitter regret. What had happened to the generous, loving, uninhibited, responsive woman he'd made love to last night?

"How much I wanted you. How good we'd be together. How much we—"

"Please," she said, her face flushed. "Don't go on. I agreed to marry you, to be your wife and all that entails to fulfill your family's wishes. I never agreed...I never would have agreed to anything more. You said..."

Exasperated, he ran his hand through his hair. "I know what I said. But I changed my mind. Did I force you, coerce you to do anything you didn't want to do?" he asked, leaning against the green-and-gold-striped wallpaper of his former guest room and piercing her with his dark eyes.

She looked away but not before he saw a flush creep up her neck and color her face. "Of course not. That's the problem. I'm weak, I admit it. I can't seem to resist you. As you probably guessed, I'm not all that experienced, and I succumbed to your considerable charms. But in the future I'm going to hold you to your promise."

"Why?" he asked.

"Why? Because sex without love is wrong. Obviously you don't agree with me. But it's what I believe, despite what I did last night. I'm not proud of myself for not living up to my belief. Even if I didn't feel that way, there are other reasons you may find easier to understand. One—" she held up one finger "—it could be a habit, falling into bed together. A bad habit. Think about it. Two—" she held up a second finger "—we have to work together. Sex will only complicate our working relationship. And three—" she held up another finger "—we're getting a divorce in one year. And then you'll pick up with one or more of your many girlfriends."

"You have it all figured out," he said harshly.

"Not all," she said, lowering her gaze to study her shoes. "But I'm working on it."

"Something's bothering you, isn't it?" he asked. "Last night…"

"Last night was a mistake. Last night is over." She stood. He could tell she wanted him to leave. She preferred unpacking to talking to him. She preferred almost anything to talking to him at this moment.

"Okay, if that's the way you want it." He looked at his watch. "What about dinner, shall we go out?"

"I don't feel like it. I could cook something if you'd like."

She was so polite he wanted to shake her. "I didn't marry you so you could be my cook. I'll order something sent in."

They made polite conversation over dinner delivered from a neighborhood French restaurant. No take-out Chinese for Emily. The least he could do was to spoil her a little. He thought of something else. No matter what she said, he hadn't given up on seducing his wife.

"I want you to go ahead with the garden on the terrace," he said glancing at the French doors that opened onto his rooftop patio.

For the first time all day she looked at him with real interest. "Are you sure? What made you change your mind?"

"It looks bare out there. I want some color, some life."

"Would you want roses?" she asked cautiously.

"Of course I want roses. But I didn't plant in the spring. I'd need a protected spot away from the wind, wouldn't I, and rich loam."

She nodded. He hoped she was impressed that he remembered her lecture on roses. At least it gave them something safe to talk about until it was bedtime. Then she went to her room. Before he went to his, he stood in the living room, with its coolly elegant modern furniture, and stared down the hall at her closed door. When he'd woken up this morning, with the imprint of her lips still on his, the scent of her hair lingering on the pillow, he'd never imagined the day would end like this.

He didn't know what to do. When it came to women he was not accustomed to being rejected. Nor when it came to business for that matter. He wanted to pursue Emily, woo her, seduce her as he would any woman who intrigued him the way she did. But would it do any good? He'd never seen such determination as he saw in her eyes, in the set of her stubborn chin. When he asked himself if she had a weakness, the answer was—roses.

But it wasn't her only weakness. For one thing she had a fondness for candy and earrings and books. So he didn't stop with roses. In the following days he left a box of dark chocolates in her In box, the kind he knew she liked, later a pair of diamond studs on her dresser, followed by a coffee-table book filled with pictures of English gardens on her desk and a new pair of gardening gloves on the terrace with her tools.

He'd never done anything like this. He'd never wanted to be bothered. In his life BE—before Emily—he'd showered his girlfriends with presents because it was expected, but it was Emily who'd picked them out, ordered them and had them delivered. Then he sat back as the women showered him with their thanks and gratitude for his thought-fulness.

Emily didn't shower him with anything. In fact, he wondered from her brief thank-yous how much she really liked anything he got her. Which just made him try harder. He sometimes left the office at noon and went shopping or ordered through catalogues. One day she came into his office with a still-unopened box from an expensive lingerie store. The look in her eyes was not one of overwhelming gratitude. She gave him a suspicious look through narrowed eyes.

"What's this?" she asked, holding it by the ribbon in front of her as if it might contain a jack-in-the-box that would jump out at her.

"Why don't you open it and see?" he asked, hiding a smile at her obvious discomfort. Wanting to see the look on her face when she saw what the box contained.

"You don't have to give me presents. I'm not one of your girlfriends."

"Do you mean only girlfriends get presents in America and not wives?" he asked. "I didn't know that. But then I've never been married before," he said.

"You know what I mean. We're married. We have a deal. I'm not going to back out on it. You don't have to pamper me."

"But I want to pamper you," he said.

"Why?"

Why? Not because he expected her to jump into bed with him on account of a gift. He wasn't that naive. Rather to see if he could make her eyes light up, to see if she'd throw her arms around him in a spontaneous burst of gratitude, to watch her blush at the sight of the negligee, to hear her murmur her thanks in his ear.

"I like giving presents," he said blandly. "So indulge me. Open the box."

She sighed as if he'd asked her to put on a silly costume and run the Bay to Breakers Race.

Clearly uneasy, she fumbled with the wrapping, had trouble untying the bow. "I wish you wouldn't do this," she murmured. "I don't need any more...oh." She ran her fingers over the exquisitely fine handmade lace peignoir. "It's beautiful. Thank you, Ben."

"You're welcome."

He didn't expect her to try it on. He didn't even expect her to hold it up against her body. But he didn't expect her to go running from the office, either. But run she did. He supposed he ought to be relieved she didn't try to give it back to him. He only hoped that someday she'd feel comfortable enough to wear it. Not for him, but for herself. To look beautiful. To feel beautiful.

He was disappointed, but not surprised to see Emily had reverted to wearing her old clothes to work. The shapeless dark suits, the skirts at mid-calf and the white blouses buttoned to the collarbone. It was almost as if there had been no wedding, no honeymoon. If they didn't ride to work together in the limo the company sent for them in the morning, and back at night, he might have thought it was all a dream.

At work her attitude was completely professional. Maybe that's why she hated to find a gift from him on her desk. Even a simple bouquet of daisies seemed to overwhelm her. If anyone else at work noticed her cool attitude toward him and the presents he gave her, and thought it odd, they accepted it. He told himself he'd have to accept it, too. He might have to accept it, but he didn't have to like it. He hated it.

He wanted to lure her into his office on some pretext,

lock the door and make love to her on the desk or the thick carpet. Anywhere. Because under those unbecoming garments she wore he knew what was there. He knew there was a warm, sensuous, incredibly responsible woman who was bottling up her natural sexuality. He saw it as an incredible waste.

Strange as it seemed, he saw more of her at work than at home. At work they both felt more comfortable. There their roles were clearly defined. At home they avoided each other. She gardened. She threw herself into the terrace project with all her considerable energy, spending so much time at garden outlets and poring over catalogs, he was almost sorry he'd suggested it.

By unspoken agreement, the terrace was her territory. He spent his evenings in his book-lined office and didn't intrude. But one night he was restless, on edge. If he didn't know better he might have thought he was lonely. But that couldn't be. He'd lived alone for years, and he'd always relished his solitude, a welcome relief from the hectic atmosphere at the office.

But he wandered out to the terrace that unseasonably warm summer evening seeking something…he didn't really know what. He just knew she'd be there. Maybe he just wanted to see her in something other than a tailored suit that didn't really fit her. Maybe he just plain wanted to see her, though he'd seen her at the office only a few hours ago.

He pushed the French doors open and stood in the doorway amazed at the transformation. In a matter of a month, she'd turned his sterile patio into an arboretum. She had climbing and rambler roses covering trellises. There were new pots of hybrid tea roses giving off a heavenly fruitlike perfume. And planters filled with low bushes bearing small clusters of blossoms. In the dusk, the deep red American Beauties took on a sensuous glow.

She was on her knees in a shrunken cotton T-shirt and old faded dungarees, a smudge of dirt on her cheek. His heart contracted. She was so damned earnest, so engaging, so charming, so unaware of how she affected him. It was all he could do to keep from crossing the patio, lifting her up to wipe that smudge off her face and kissing her.

Instead he forced himself to speak in a casual tone. "Need any help?"

Her head jerked up, and she dropped her trowel. "Oh, I didn't see you. I'm trying to transplant this Rubiayat into a bigger container, but the roots are so heavy and deep..." She frowned, and he crossed the patio, kneeled down beside her and picked up the trowel.

In a few minutes he'd dug it up and had it nestled in the large terra-cotta pot. Together they filled the pot, around the roots, from a large sack of potting soil. Occasionally his fingers touched hers in the dirt, but she appeared not to notice the contact. When they finished, she brushed her hands together.

"Thank you," she said.

"Why didn't you tell me you needed help?"

"I thought you were working. I didn't want to bother you."

He took her hands in his and helped her to her feet. "There are times when I want to be bothered," he muttered. He tightened his grip on her hands, dirt and all and looked into her cloud-gray eyes. Working together here at home, making physical contact, was very different from working together at the office, and he didn't want to break the mood. Maybe it was the scent of the flowers. Maybe it was the look in her eyes. The touch of her hands.

He didn't want to let go of her or to go back inside. It

made him wonder if perhaps he'd missed something all these years of bachelorhood. The everyday intimacy of marriage. The contact, both physical and emotional. She was getting to be a habit with him. A dangerous habit, because the last thing he wanted was to change his lifestyle and tie himself down. Thank God she'd still be his assistant at the end of the year. That way he'd have the best of both worlds. His freedom and Emily, too.

Just for good measure he reminded himself of the obligations of marriage and even of a garden. You had to hire a gardener, you had to have someone come in and water if you were gone.... Yes, he'd made the right decision. Wives required even more care than gardens. Not Emily, of course. She was different. She was definitely a low-maintenance wife. But then, she was not his real wife.

"You've done a beautiful job here. I don't know how I got along without a garden before. By the way, who's taking care of the garden at your house?"

"Peggy is, with some help from the other club members. Which reminds me, they want to see the terrace. Is there a time when—"

"Anytime. Oh, a time when I wouldn't be here, is that what you mean? I won't embarrass you, if that's what you're afraid of. It's a big apartment, you won't even know I'm here."

"That's not what I'm afraid of. The club is almost as interested in seeing you as my roses," Emily said. "I just didn't want to inconvenience you." Which was a lie. She just didn't want her friends to see that she was living a lie. She could see it now. The women oohing and aahing over the apartment. Just dying for a glimpse of her handsome husband, the sheik. They'd ask questions, they'd try to imagine what her life was like and they'd be wrong, so wrong, no matter what they thought, because no one could imagine what her life was like. How compartmentalized. How phony. And then what if one of them would stumble into her room by mistake and wonder why she had her own room, her own bed, her own— She realized he was still holding her hand, still gazing into her eyes, and she broke away.

"Inconvenience me? Emily, you've known me for over three years. Am I the type who'd let someone inconvenience them without saying something? Don't you always know how I feel and what I want? Do I strike you as some kind of ogre? Never mind, don't answer that. On your garden club night I'll go to the Olympic Club and play cards or whatever it was I used to do."

"Don't do that. If you want to go to your club, you can go anytime. I certainly don't mind. After all..."

"I know what you're going to say, 'After all, it's not a real marriage.'" His jaw was clamped tight, and his voice was strained.

"Well, is it?" she countered.

"It could be," he said with a pointed look at her that was meant to remind her of that night, the first night they'd spent under this roof. The last night they'd spent truly together under this roof. His eyes smoldered. Her knees weakened. She reached for the trellis to brace herself. She knew exactly what he meant.

"For how long, a year? That's not a real marriage." How could he possibly think she'd sleep with him for a year and then walk away as if nothing had happened? Just one night had been enough to show her how hard it would be. Not just hard. Impossible. But not for him. He was accustomed to love-'em-and-leave-'em relationships. For a week, a month or a year. He'd always been able to walk away, leaving the woman with a dozen long-stemmed roses or an expensive bauble or both. With her he'd started the gift-giving early. Every time he gave her something it reminded her of the fragility of their marriage. How it was programmed to end in one year, and the thought made her unutterably sad.

But he didn't know that. He thought that was how it was done. Giving presents had always worked for him in the past. It ensured there'd be no hard feelings. Everyone came out ahead. Everyone won. No one lost. If she were one of those women...but she wasn't.

"Have it your way, Emily," he said abruptly, and the discussion was over. He walked to the parapet and looked out across the city to the graceful bridge that spanned the bay.

She stood there, one hand still gripping the trellis, looking at him, unable to tear her eyes from his broad shoulders in a blue polo shirt, his narrow hips in khakis. Every day he got better looking, whether at home or at the office. Every day she wanted him more. Wanted to believe that the things he gave her were gifts from the heart and not offerings to appease her, to pave the way for the eventual breakup. She desperately wanted to feel his arms around her, his lips on hers. Wanted to share his bed, his life. Not just for a year, but for always. Knowing that it was never going to happen hurt like a knife in her chest.

Every day she felt like she was falling deeper and deeper into a hole that she wouldn't be able to climb out of. Every day she loved him more than the day before. If she'd known it would be like this, she never would have agreed to this scheme. If only she hadn't slept with him. It would still be bad, but not this bad. There would be pain, but not this constant ache deep inside her, a hollow feeling that would never be filled. She'd tasted heaven in his arms and now she was paying the price. It was hell.

He seemed to have forgotten she was there. But something made her walk over and join him. Maybe it was the realization that they were in this together, that it might be just as hard for him to be locked into a false marriage for a year as it was for her. For completely different reasons. That he might be lonely too, more lonely than when he lived alone. Just as she was.

She followed his gaze as the lights came on over the city. From far away came the muted traffic sounds of the city. Only a few inches remained between them. When he put his arm around her shoulders and drew her to him, she didn't resist. She couldn't. It seemed so natural to have her shoulder rest against his arm, her hip nestled against his.

"Thank you," he said gruffly.

"For what?" She held her breath. She was afraid he was going to thank her for marrying him.

"For this, this garden. I never knew what I was missing."

"I could leave them all here for you when I go."

"Are you counting the days?" he asked. He kept his arm around her shoulders, but she felt him draw away from her in a deeper sense.

"No, of course not. I'm very comfortable here." Liar. She'd never been more uncomfortable. No matter how big his apartment was, she could hear his footsteps, smell his aftershave, see him at the breakfast table, so close and yet so far. She knew he wanted her, though she didn't know why, because she wasn't his type. But he wanted her, anyway. It made her feel good, it made her feel desirable, but it made her feel bad, too. She knew what bliss it would be to spend every night in his arms, but she'd always wonder who would be next.

"You'd better take them with you," he said, returning to the safer subject of the flowers. "I don't know how to take care of a garden. And frankly I couldn't be bothered.

I got along without them before, I'll manage to get along without them after they're gone.''

The significance of the statement hit Emily like an arrow through the heart. If he could get along without the flowers, he could just as easily get along without her. Taking care of flowers was just like taking care of a wife. He just didn't want to be bothered. Yes, he'd get along fine without her, but she was not going to find it so easy to get along without him. Unless she was very very careful.

''No, the plants would wither away without your care,'' he continued. As if he hadn't said enough so far. ''You have a way with them. It's obvious you're the nurturing, care-giving kind.''

She nodded and slipped out from under his arm. She didn't trust herself to get close to him, physically or emotionally. He was a threat to her willpower. A danger to her fragile state of well-being. A constant reminder of how little she meant to him as anything but a gardener or his assistant. She pressed her hand against her heart to stop the pounding and went to take refuge in her room.

Chapter Nine

Days went by with only minimal contact between them both at home, whereas at the office they were frantically busy working together on a new drilling site in Central Asia. One day during the next week he called her into his office. He was all business. Until he told her what he wanted.

"I know you're busy working on the Tenghiz Basin project for me, but I have to interrupt. I just had a call from my cousin Ahmed."

"Did I meet him at the wedding?"

"No, he wasn't at the wedding. He was sorry to miss it, but his wife just had a baby. We grew up close as brothers and he went to school with me at Berkeley. He too is married to an American."

"How nice."

He glanced up at her, his sharp eyes missing nothing. She was sorry if she'd sounded sarcastic. It *was* nice that his cousin was married. What else could she say?

"I assume he doesn't know about us, about our agreement?"

"He knows I'm married, that's all. I would like him to think it's for real. Because if word got back..."

"I understand," she murmured.

"They are in town and want to see us. Knowing me, they were surprised to hear I finally broke down and got married. They're curious to see who finally changed my mind."

"I hope they won't be disappointed," she said, tiny worry lines etched in her forehead.

"Why should they be?"

"I'm not glamorous or beautiful," she said matter-of-factly.

"Who told you you weren't beautiful?" he said, coming out from behind his desk.

"No one told me. They didn't have to. I looked in the mirror. It doesn't matter. I don't care."

"I do," he said, crossing the room to face her. He tilted her chin and forced her to look at him. "What can I do to convince you otherwise?" He leaned forward as if he was going to kiss her, and she rocked back on her heels. She mustn't let him talk to her like that. She mustn't let him say those things. And most of all she mustn't let him kiss her.

She swallowed hard. "About your cousin," she said.

"Oh, yes." He drew his eyebrows together as if he was going to say, what cousin? With a visible effort, he turned and went back to his desk. "He was sorry to miss the wedding, and they've heard about you from the family, so naturally they want to meet you. Congratulate us, et cetera, et cetera. I suggested dinner tomorrow night at the Fleur de Lys if that's convenient for you."

The Fleur de Lys, an elegant French restaurant, one of Ben's favorites. "Will they be bringing their baby?"

"Their baby?" he asked. "I guess so, why?"

"Because the Fleur de Lys is not a good place to take a baby. Why don't we invite them to your apartment, then they can bring the baby. I'll cook something. It won't be as fancy as the restaurant, but it might reinforce the illusion that we're really married, if that's what you want."

He shrugged. "If you think so. But I didn't marry you to get a cook. Besides, I thought you were busy."

"I am busy, but for the moment I'm at a standstill. It's a national holiday in Khasakistan, so nothing's happening right now. You know, sometimes I get tired of ordering out every night. You have a beautiful kitchen and we never use it. I have a recipe for veal scallopini I used to make for the garden club. If you don't mind my taking the afternoon off tomorrow, I'd like to make it for them."

"You can take the afternoon off whenever you want. In fact I was going to tell you to take some time off when you could. You've been working too hard. It's my fault. I've given you too much responsibility." He frowned at her. "You have circles under your eyes."

She brushed her fingers across her face as if she could banish the circles. If he only knew the reason for the circles. It was not the work at the office. It was living with him. If he knew how hard it was to sleep under the same roof with him. To watch the minutes tick by and the hours. Knowing that her time was running out. Slowly but surely. Oh, it wouldn't be over for some months, but still...

"All right," he said. "I'll call and invite them."

She paused at the door. "Tell them to bring the baby," she said. She didn't know why it was so important. She just knew she wanted to see the child. And hold it if they'd let her. She told herself it was the least she could do. Showing them Ben's marriage was for real. She'd even dress up, wear makeup maybe. Then they wouldn't be so shocked when they saw her. She could just hear them as they left the apartment after dinner.

She's not what we expected, but she's nice enough.

Ben always said he'd never get married, so there must be something there that doesn't meet the eye.

She's a good cook.

She likes children.

Her garden was beautiful.

Yes, they could say those things. She hoped they would. Because that's why she was making the effort, wasn't it? Or was it really for Ben? If she was honest with herself wouldn't she admit that she wanted Ben to know she was a good cook and that she liked children? Even though she knew it didn't matter to him. All he really cared about was how she did her jobs—her job as his assistant and her job as his wife. That was the sad truth.

Oh, yes, he wanted to make love to her. But she knew why. It was because she was there. She was convenient. He couldn't go out with other women. He wouldn't do that while he was married to her, so what choice did he have? It was abstinence or her. Knowing this made it easier to say no. But not so easy that she wasn't counting the days until this marriage was over. He was right about that.

Though not as handsome, Ben's cousin looked a lot like him, and his wife was an all-American girl named Joanne, with blond hair and blue eyes. Their baby was beautiful with fine dark hair and huge dark eyes like her father's. They put her down for a nap in Ben's bedroom, and she fell asleep immediately before Emily had had a chance to hold her.

With a wistful backward glance at the sleeping baby,

Emily regretfully closed the bedroom door and took them on a tour of her terrace garden.

Ben told them about their visit to the Butchart Gardens, and Emily described the characteristics of different roses and how she chose them with the terrace and its western exposure in mind. She was surprised to hear Ben tell them how and when to plant roses and which were the hardiest. She hadn't realized he'd picked up so much information from her.

Ahmed and his wife exchanged significant looks. "It's beautiful," Joanne said, bending over to sniff a Mamie Eisenhower rose. "How do you have time to garden when Ben keeps you working all day at the office?"

"On weekends, of course, and then sometimes I leave work early," Emily explained. "Ben is a very understanding boss."

"And husband," he said, putting his arm around her.

"Yes, of course," she said, her voice a little shaky, the color rising in her face. Was this really necessary? she wondered.

"Can you believe this is your cousin?" Joanne asked her husband. "The man who said he'd never put down roots."

"Not really roots," Emily said, lest they get the wrong idea entirely. "I mean everything's in pots. It can all be moved."

"That's good, because one of these days you'll want to leave the city. When you have kids you'll realize it's no place to raise a child."

Emily didn't dare to even glance at Ben. She looked at her watch and hurriedly excused herself to go to the kitchen, as if something might be burning. Something was burning. It was her face. Joanne followed her, and Emily put her to work slicing cucumbers. Then to distract Joanne from talking about her and Ben, she asked how Joanne had met her husband.

"It was a party at the International House. But at first I was afraid to get involved with him," Joanne confided to Emily. "I thought if I married him I'd have to wear a veil and live in his country. But he and Ben loved it here. They'd already made up their minds to stay in the U.S. And so here we are." She smiled so brightly, so happily, that Emily's heart was filled with envy. This was no sham marriage. They had the baby to prove it.

"What about you and Ben? You said you'd worked at Oil International for three years. How come it took you so long to discover each other? Ben is so good-looking and so charming."

"Yes, well…" Emily had no answer for that one. She could say that it didn't take her long to discover Ben's charm. It took her just about two months before she'd fallen head-over-heels for him. It wasn't just his good looks, he was always so kind and considerate of her. He still was. Nothing had changed. Except for a piece of paper called a marriage certificate. He didn't feel any different from her than he ever had.

"I confess that when we lived in the city I set Ben up with all my unmarried friends at one time or another," Joanne continued. "Now I know why he didn't go for any of them. He was waiting for you."

Emily blushed. "I don't think so," she said, pouring dressing on the salad. "I think it was just a matter of timing. He's almost thirty-five, you know, and he was feeling some pressure from his family. I was available and so…"

"But I can tell the way he looks at you this is true love."

Emily opened her mouth to protest, but realized it was fruitless. People believed what they wanted to believe, no matter what evidence there was to the contrary.

Meanwhile in the living room in front of the picture window, Ben poured a glass of sparkling grape juice for his cousin.

"I can't believe it," Ahmed said, shaking his head. "You, married. I can see now why you waited. She's a lovely girl."

"Yes, she is."

"And so much in love with you."

"You think so?" Ben asked dubiously.

"Of course. I saw the way she looked at you. Why else would she have married you?"

"For my money?" Ben suggested, hoping his cousin didn't guess he was serious. She had married him for his money. And to help him out of a jam. But basically it was the thought of getting her greenhouse that had swayed her.

"Not Emily. Some of your other women, maybe. But she's not the type. I can see it in her face." He shook his head. "No, she's got it bad for you, cousin. I'm not blind, you know."

Ben frowned. He wasn't blind, either, and he certainly would have noticed if Emily was…no, it wasn't possible. Thank heavens. It would be damned awkward if either of them got that attached to the other.

"Of course that doesn't surprise me," Ahmed continued. "Girls falling in love with you is not exactly unusual. What I can't believe is that you, you who swore you'd never get married, you're as much in love with her as she is with you."

"Right," Ben said. "How did you know?"

"You've got that look in your eyes. Don't try to deny it. I know you better than you know yourself. You should see yourself, following her everywhere with your eyes. The way you talk about her. The first time you mentioned her on the phone, your voice was different. I heard it. You're in love, all right."

"Really," Ben said. His cousin had apparently gone completely off his rocker. It must be fatherhood that had done it. He used to be just as caustic and cynical as Ben.

"Yes, really."

Later, over dinner in Ben's formal dining room, which he said he never used until he got married, Ben and his cousin reminisced about the good times they had growing up. Riding horses across the desert sands, sailing in the Gulf...

"I taught Emily to sail on our honeymoon," Ben said proudly.

"What about riding?" his cousin asked.

"Not yet," Ben said. "We've only been married a month." He looked across the table at Emily, caught her eye and held her gaze for a long moment. One month and they'd sailed, worked together, traveled, played together but made love only once. No one would believe it if they knew. Emily blushed as if she knew what he was thinking. But what was *she* thinking? One month down and eleven to go?

"How do you manage," Joanne asked Emily, "being his assistant at work and being his wife at home? I mean, do you ever forget where you are and close the door to his office and—"

Emily dropped her fork. "Never," she said quickly.

Ben smothered a smile. How often he'd wanted to do that very thing. Just knowing she was in her office, only steps away, sent his heart pounding at the possibilities. Locking the door behind them, tearing those shapeless suits off her delectable body, and making love to her on the long leather couch. Seeing sensible, level-headed Emily blush and get flustered across the dinner table made him wonder if she ever allowed herself to have the same fantasies. He grinned at her. She studiously avoided his gaze.

"Actually we see more of each other at work than at home," Ben explained. How true. At work their relationship was firmly defined, whereas at home they skirted around each other, afraid to invade each other's space, afraid of not quite knowing what to say or how to act.

Ahmed raised his eyebrows. "Really?"

"What I mean is, we have a great working relationship. I couldn't get along without her," Ben said firmly.

"You may have to, someday," Joanne said.

Emily bit her lip. Ben frowned. He knew he'd have to get along without Emily as a wife at the end of the year, but he didn't ever plan on giving up Emily as his assistant.

"When you have children," Joanne explained with a smile. "You'll want to spend more time at home. Even though you love your job. Just think, next year at this time you may be expecting…"

Emily paled. She opened her mouth to say something. Ben nudged her under the table as a warning. This was a case where it was best to say nothing. She closed her mouth, and Ben exhaled. They'd jumped over another hurdle.

Just then the baby woke up and started to cry. It was the most welcome sound of the evening.

Joanne returned to the table with the baby in her arms. Emily offered to hold her while Joanne finished her dinner.

"Are you sure you don't mind?" Joanne asked.

Eagerly Emily held out her arms. Ben watched her lift the baby into her arms and impulsively press her lips into the soft black curls on the baby's head. Her eyes were meltingly soft. The look on her face was one of pure longing. Ben was surprised. He'd never thought Emily would want to be a mother. And yet it figured. She was a nurturer, a tender of plants. She raised flowers. She could raise children. She'd be a great mother. If that was what she wanted. From the look on her face, it was.

Ahmed helped himself to a third helping of veal while Joanne smiled at the sight of her baby in Emily's arms. Ben smiled, too, but his heart contracted at the picture they made, his wife and the baby. He felt a shaft of envy pierce his heart. He scarcely recognized it. He'd never envied anyone. Not his cousin, not anyone. He had everything he'd ever wanted. But he realized in one sense he had nothing compared to Ahmed. Nothing compared to a wife and a baby.

A wife and a baby? He must be crazy. He didn't even want the responsibility of a garden. Not until now, anyway.

Ben was almost glad when they got ready to leave. He was torn apart with conflicting emotions. Seeing Emily with the baby, watching her serve dinner, hearing that she was in love with him, and then pretending this was a real marriage. It took a huge effort.

He watched Emily reluctantly give up the baby and they said goodbye at the door. He closed the door behind them and breathed a sigh of relief. It wasn't easy fending off questions about love and babies. Emily dropped into the sectional sofa as if she was so tired her legs couldn't hold her any longer. She closed her eyes. He wasn't the only one making an effort to fool his relatives. Maybe she was sorry they hadn't gone to the Fleur de Lys after all. They might have been able to steer the conversation a little better. Avoid those embarrassing topics.

"You must have inherited the Claybourne acting talent after all," he said.

Her eyes flew open. "How do you mean?"

"Ahmed swears you're in love with me. He said he

could see it in your face. Isn't that ridiculous? As if I wouldn't know if you were in love with me.''

''Ridiculous,'' she agreed. ''Here's what's funny. Joanne told me she thinks you're in love with me.'' Her mouth turned up in an attempt at a smile, but it never reached her eyes. Instead he could have sworn her eyes were glazed with tears.

''Go to bed,'' he said. ''I'll clean up.'' He was afraid if she stayed any longer, he might say something he'd be sorry for.

She didn't protest. She got to her feet. Before she left the room, he asked a question. ''Have you ever thought of having children, Emily?''

''No,'' she said. ''Why do you ask?''

''For a moment when you were holding my niece I thought…''

''I don't intend to have children,'' she said stiffly. ''My life is full enough the way it is. I have all I can handle—taking care of roses and working full-time, besides you have to be married to have children, and I—''

''You are not really married. You don't have to say it. You should be glad you're not. Husbands require a great deal of attention. Even more than roses.''

''Not you,'' she said. ''You require less care than any plant.''

He smiled sardonically. ''Thank you.''

''Besides—''

''Emily, if you say this isn't a real marriage one more time…''

''It isn't.''

He clenched his jaw so tightly he was afraid it would be locked into place. Fortunately he could still speak. Because he wasn't finished with her. He was so angry he wanted to shake her. ''Do you know why it isn't?'' he demanded.

"It's because we have separate bedrooms. It's because I want to make love to you, and I think you want to make love with me. I'm not going to ask you or tempt you to share my bed, Emily. You've made your position clear to me. But if you change your mind, you have only to let me know. I won't be holding my breath, because for some reason…"

"For some reason?" she said, her eyes blazing, her cheeks bright with spots of color. "The reason is that despite what anyone says, you're not in love with me and I'm not in love with you, and I'm not going to make love with anyone who doesn't love me. All right, I did it once, but I can't do it again. It goes against everything I believe in. Maybe it doesn't matter to you. Obviously it doesn't. I don't know how you felt about all those other women in your life. Maybe you were in love with them and maybe they were in love with you, but I doubt it."

"Of course not. I believe we've had this discussion before. You know my feelings about love."

"You don't think it exists," Emily said. "How can you say that, when you've just spent the evening in the company of your cousin and his wife. Do you deny that they're in love?"

He shrugged. "It's immaterial. You see you've just proved my theory of what's required in a marriage. Do you deny they have mutual respect and admiration?" he asked.

"No, of course not," she said. "I agree they have it, and I agree it's important. But it's not enough. Not enough to last a lifetime. There has to be something else."

"I know what you're going to say," he said, shaking his head. "It's love, isn't it? When are you going to give up that romantic notion?"

"Never," she said. "And don't tell me love doesn't exist," she said. "Because I know it does."

"From personal experience?" he asked, raising one eyebrow.

"Yes," she said. Then she wrenched herself from his grip and stomped down the hall to her bedroom and slammed the door behind her.

Ben stood in the middle of the living room with his arms crossed over his waist. The sound of the door slamming reverberated in the sudden silence. He'd never heard Emily raise her voice. Never known her to slam a door. He was dumbfounded. He thought they were having a rational discussion and all of a sudden she went to pieces.

He paced back and forth trying to figure out what set her off like that. Not that he wasn't angry, too. But he didn't walk out on her or slam any doors. Of all the women in the world, why did he have to marry this one? And why, if he was married to her, why wouldn't she make love with him? What could be more moral than making love with your husband? Not only moral but legal, too.

She seemed to like and respect him, but she didn't love him. And he didn't love her. What was wrong with that? The thing that perplexed him was that she said she'd had personal experience with love. Now what was that all about? He had half a mind to knock on her door and ask her. But he didn't. He sat down and stretched his legs out in front of him and stared into space.

Love, that overrated emotion. He never wanted to hear the word again.

Emily was not going to cry herself to sleep. She'd shed too many tears over Ben already. If she stayed awake that night it was to worry whether or not she'd said too much. She realized now that she'd almost given her secret away. She also realized that a one-sided love was worse than no love at all. If she hadn't given him her word, if she hadn't

signed that contract, she'd walk out of there and go back
to her house. Her safe haven. Then she'd only have to face
Ben eight hours a day. She still liked working for him. They
understood each other perfectly. Finished each other's sen-
tences. Fed on each other's enthusiasms. Why couldn't it
be like that at home?

The next day things were back to normal, at least at the
office. Until his father called from his oil-rich sheikdom in
the Gulf. Ben was in a meeting, so Emily took the call. Her
palm was damp as she gripped the receiver. She was afraid
he'd ask her if she'd fallen in love with Ben yet, or if she
was pregnant yet. But he didn't.

"Emily, my dear. I have good news. As Ben has perhaps
told you, my wife and I are celebrating our fiftieth wedding
anniversary."

"No, no, he didn't. Congratulations."

"No, not yet. Save your congratulations until next
month. The good news is that we are throwing a party for
ourselves, and we are sending you and Ben plane tickets.
So you can't say that you're too busy. It will be your first
time to see our homeland. And participate in our annual
ceremony of the renewal of vows."

Emily didn't say they were too busy. She didn't say anything at all. She had no idea what to say. She didn't know
if Ben wanted her to see his homeland or participate in a
ceremony. She didn't want to ask him and hear him beat
around the bush, not wanting to hurt her feelings, but not
wanting her there, either. Most of all she didn't want to ask
what a renewal of vows consisted of. When his father called
back later, she happened to be in Ben's office poring over
some blueprints for worker housing at the new oil-well site.

When Ben picked up the phone, she walked softly to the
door and quickly escaped just as she heard his father's
voice over the speaker phone.

"I've already spoken to Emily," his father said. "And she has agreed so it's all set."

"What's all set, Father?" Ben asked with a frown, glancing at the door Emily had just closed behind her. Why hadn't she told him? It wasn't like her to forget to give him a message.

"You're coming to the festivities to celebrate our fiftieth anniversary. Nothing elaborate, you understand."

"What, no camel races, no trained falcons?" Ben asked.

"Well, perhaps just a few," his father admitted. "But mostly it's a chance for ourselves and our married children, of whom you are now a part," his father said pointedly, "to renew their solemn wedding vows."

"We just took our vows," Ben protested. "Don't you think it's too soon for a renewal?"

"You took your vows in America. I understand that. It's your home now. But this is still the land of your birth. There are many relatives who haven't met your bride."

His bride. Relatives who wanted to meet his bride. Wait until Emily heard about this. Or had she already heard?

"So father, you've already cleared this with Emily?"

"Just this morning. Now, can we count on you?"

"I suppose, but..."

"No buts, I'm having the plaque engraved today. The one with our names on it and yours and the date of your wedding. What is Emily's middle name, by the way?"

"I don't know."

"You don't know?"

Father, there are so many things I don't know about her. Her dreams, her hopes for the future. So many things I can't ask her. Because you see, this is just a temporary arrangement. I know you think we'll fall in love with each other, but it's not going to happen. For one thing, I don't believe in love and another...

"Ask her and get back to me," his father said.

"Yes, all right." Ben hung up and braced his elbows on his desk. Guilt and resentment warred within him. His father's words reverberated through his head. The plaque. The names. The wedding. Ceremony was very important in his culture.

He loved his father. He loved the whole family, but they were going too far this time. He'd never heard of a renewal of vows ceremony and he wondered if his father had just invented it in an attempt to cement his marriage—if perhaps his father was worried he might try to back out of the marriage at the end of the year. Which of course he would. He didn't want to tell Emily about this next hurdle. No matter what she'd told his father, he was sure she'd feel awkward at such a ceremony. But he had to tell her. Now. He had to prevail on her to do this for him. They had to put up a united front. Or this whole marriage would be for nothing.

Chapter Ten

The plane landed in the small oil-rich sheikdom on the Arabian Gulf and two passengers emerged from the first-class cabin into the intense heat and humidity. Emily and Ben were met by the family chauffeur in an air-conditioned Mercedes 300 and driven directly to the Mansour family compound an hour away.

During the drive Ben kept up a running commentary, describing the small villages and outdoor marketplaces they passed and the hydroponic farms that provided fresh vegetables to the population of this dry, sandy desert.

Emily made appropriate comments and asked questions. All the while her stomach was doing nervous flip-flops inside and she was asking herself why she had come. Ben had told her it was up to her. He wouldn't insist. After all, a trip to the Arabian Gulf was not part of the bargain. Neither was participating in a renewal of their vows. But she felt a sense of obligation. Both to Ben and to his family. And she had to admit that she was curious about his homeland.

Despite their arguments on the existence of love, and the impossibility of his ever falling in love with anyone, let alone her, Emily was determined to finish out the year. It was what she'd promised and she would see it through, no matter how painful it was. So now she was here and this ceremony was looming. Ben told her it was nothing to worry about, but she heard the tension in his voice, saw the lines tighten around his mouth when he told her about it. If there was nothing to worry about, why was he so worried?

The car turned, crossed the sand dunes and entered the gate into a veritable oasis. A villa of Italian marble stood at the center, surrounded by green grass and olive trees. Emily's eyes widened at the sight of the low buildings built on the shores of the dazzling blue waters of the Gulf. Speechless with delight, she was escorted from the car by dozens of family members wearing traditional robes and headdress.

"You must be Emily," an old woman said in heavily accented English. "Welcome to our family."

And so it went, until she'd been embraced by every cousin, every aunt and uncle of the large, extended family. She felt the warmth of their reception came from their hearts, and some of her fear of not measuring up, of disappointing them by being from the wrong culture, melted away. Now she only had to fear fooling them into thinking their marriage was forever. She was looking forward to seeing his cousin Ahmed, his wife and baby who would be arriving the next day.

"They're wonderful people," Emily said after a servant had shown them to their room. The bed, covered with a filmy netting and standing in the center of the room, was right out of the *Arabian Nights*. She swallowed a wistful sigh. Yes, she knew she'd have to share a bed with Ben.

After all, she didn't expect to find two beds set up for them when they were still honeymooners, as his father so pointedly reminded them. But she also knew they would each lie on their own side, like strangers who were playing roles. Because Ben was going to wait for her to make the next move. And that would never happen.

"You're wonderful, too," Ben said. "I want you to know how much I appreciate your going through with this. Everyone loves you."

Except you, she thought. But despite the fact that Ben didn't love her, or maybe because of it, she basked in the approval of his family. In the days preceding the ceremony she also basked in the hot rays of the Arabian sun. After the foggy San Francisco summer, she peeled away layers of warm clothing and let the sun gild her pale skin. They went sailing from the jetty in front of the villa, swam in the oval-shaped pool overlooking the Gulf, played croquet on the lawn with his little cousins and went horseback riding on the beach.

Suntanned, wind-blown and more relaxed than she could ever remember being, she slid off the gentle mare Ben had selected for her and landed in his arms.

His arms went around her and he kissed her lightly on the lips. "Am I mistaken or are you feeling almost more at home here than I am?" he asked, holding her at arm's length to study her face.

"I love it here," she said simply. She hadn't meant to fall in love with his home and his family, but she had.

He nodded. "This place agrees with you. There's a sparkle in your eyes, and a lilt to your smile. You look sensational, you know. Everyone has noticed. Including me."

She met his gaze, and her pulse raced when she saw the look in his eyes. She noted the lines had disappeared from his forehead, the tension gone from his mouth. She had to ball her hands into fists to keep from running her fingers along his jawline, to feel the shadow of his beard against her skin.

When he looked at her like that she felt beautiful. She felt loved and cherished. Even though she knew it wasn't so. Oh, his family loved her, but not Ben. As if it made any difference. At the end of the year she would no longer be a part of this loving family. She would still be a part of her own family, but there she was taken for granted. She was good old Emily. The sane, sensible one. Here she had become someone special. An exotic creature from America.

Parties were held every evening before the ceremony, with food on huge buffet tables that stretched from one end of the room to the other. One night there was a special dinner of barbecued lamb and couscous and stuffed dates and platters of eggplant and goat cheese.

Ben filled a plate with delicacies and brought it to her. "How are you holding up under all this?" he asked, steering her to a table for two under an awning. "You had a look in your eyes just then, sadness…regret?"

"No. I was just thinking how much my family would love this and wishing they could be here. It's like the set for *Twelfth Night* or *A Midsummer Night's Dream.*"

"Wouldn't they be proud of the way you're playing your role?" he asked.

"I don't know. Maybe you're right. Maybe I have inherited some of the Claybourne acting talent after all."

"You've certainly inherited their good looks."

She opened her mouth to protest, but he put his fingers against her lips. The gentle pressure set her heart hammering. "I'm not the only one who thinks so. Everyone has been telling me I married a beauty. Everyone tells me that marriage agrees with me."

Emily studied his face, relaxed and bronzed from the

summer sun. Yes, if she didn't know better, she too would think that it was marriage that agreed with him. When actually it was…what was it, she wondered. What made him seem so happy?

He stayed happy until the morning of the ceremony, their last day before the flight home. She stayed happy, too. Until the last day. The day of the ceremony. Then the reality of the situation hit them both like the pipe on one of the oil derricks. Time dragged by as they thought of the lies they'd have to tell. The lie they were living. The charade they were playing. They didn't talk about it. They didn't talk at all. They avoided each other, seeking the company of others. Back in their room they dressed in silence. He in his tux, she in her wedding dress like all the other wives.

The minutes dragged by. Four o'clock, four-thirty. The heat intensified, the humidity rose until the air couldn't hold another drop of moisture without turning into rain. When the wedding ritual finally took place at five in the afternoon, the air was like a wet blanket.

His parents had wanted the sacrament to be the highlight of the festivities, the meaningful and solemn occasion that no one would forget. They'd erected a huge octagonal tent of alternating blue and white silk panels which protected the participants from the sun and allowed the breezes off the Gulf to blow through it. In the middle was a circle of mosaic tiles for the participants to stand and repeat their vows. His father, in his traditional red fez with the black tassel, took him by the shoulders and murmured something to him in Arabic. He answered automatically without really knowing what he'd said.

Emily was lovely in her wedding dress. More beautiful than any wife there, more beautiful than any wife anywhere. And she was his. His wife. Ben couldn't take his eyes off her. He held her hand, and the silk and organza brushed against his skin, as soft as a caress. Memories of their wedding day came rushing back. The vows, the kiss. A small orchestra played a traditional song on a harp, a hammer dulcimer and an oud. Ben's heart sped up as their turn approached, as each couple ahead of them repeated the words that bound them together. Forever.

Her cheek was pale under her golden suntan. He tightened his grip on her hand. Afraid she might bolt, afraid the words would stick in his throat, the lies he had to tell in order not to break his father's heart.

And then it was their turn. He said the words in his own language, then in English. He promised to love and cherish her forever. He heard her do the same. And he knew, in that moment, what he'd always known since the day he'd proposed to her, that he didn't want his marriage to end in a year. He wanted it to be forever.

He felt a huge weight fall off his shoulders. He wanted to laugh or cry and shout his feelings to the world. He kissed his wife with all the passion he'd been bottling up for the past month. Again, just as at his first wedding, he felt the shock waves rock her body as his lips met hers. Her eyes were full of questions. He wanted to tell her, ask her, beg her to be his forever.

The rites were over and one hundred doves were released into the air. There were tears and laughter and hugs. Emily was pulled away from him by an aunt or maybe a cousin and he felt like he'd lost his arm or his leg. No, it was his heart they'd taken away. He looked for her, but the old women of the family had dragged her away to shower her with the traditional wedding gifts of his country—salt and bread.

Then there was dancing, the men in one circle and the women in another. And he couldn't get to her. Another feast, an ice sculpture in the middle, of swans, the birds who mate for life. Where was she, his wife? He had to find Emily, to tell her... But his father wanted to speak to him, his mother wanted to say goodbye, and by the time he got back to their room she was asleep on her side of the bed. He didn't have the heart to wake her. He could wait. He'd been waiting for years. He could wait until tomorrow.

The plane was crowded, they waved goodbye from their seats in first class, and Emily slept most of the way, so he decided to wait a little longer. For the right place and the right time. He couldn't sleep. He was too restless, too anxious. He planned what to say.

We're good together.

We get along. At work and at home.

I want you and I think you want me.

I like being married. I didn't think I would but I do. I want to stay married. I don't want it to end.

He pictured her response. Her smile. Her tears. Her happy tears. They'd take another honeymoon. A real honeymoon. Restlessly he walked up and down the aisle of the plane while she continued to sleep. How could she sleep when he couldn't?

They arrived at the apartment in the middle of the night. He carried their bags into the living room and dropped them in the middle of the floor. He didn't turn on the lights. That way the view of the glittering city and the illuminated bridge was more spectacular.

She picked up the mail and turned to go to her room.

"Wait. I want to talk to you."

She turned and yawned. How could she still be tired after sleeping on the plane? "Can't it wait until tomorrow, Ben?"

"No." He blocked her way. "We haven't talked for a day and a half. Not since the ceremony."

"What is there to say?" she asked. He couldn't say for sure, but he thought she was trembling.

"This. I want to extend our contract. I want to tear it up and start all over. Because I want to stay married to you forever. Till death do us part. I can only ask you, beg you, and hope that you feel the same."

Emily's face paled, the room spun around and she thought she would faint for sure. Of all the things he might have said, that was the last thing she expected. He wanted to marry her for real. But why?

"Why, Ben?" she asked.

"Why? Because I need you, I want you for my wife. Forever. I can't get along without you."

"But I'll be around. I'll still be your assistant."

"I don't want an assistant. I can always get an assistant. But I can't get another wife. Not like you."

"It was the ceremony, wasn't it?" she asked. "It made you feel guilty. You made a vow and now you feel you have to keep it."

"No. Yes, that's part of it. The ceremony made me stop and think. Made me realize what I wanted. But that's not all. It's you. You're the one I want. Forever. Tell me you want me, too, forever."

She stood listening, waiting in vain for the words she'd never hear. That he loved her. Finally after a long silence, after he stood waiting with his hands clenched at his sides, she spoke.

"I do want you," she admitted, "but I can't marry someone who doesn't love me, who doesn't even believe in love."

"Why does it matter so much?" he asked, his forehead furrowed.

"Because being married to you has made me realize how important love is. It's made me realize there's something missing in our arrangement. Yes, I know what you think it is. But it isn't that. It's love. Your parents have it, your cousin has it. Every happy couple has love. And I want it, too. I used to think it was out of my reach, but now I don't. Do you know why?''

He stood staring at her, his eyes narrowed, and finally he shook his head.

''Because of you. You've made me feel cherished, you've made me feel special and beautiful and worthy of love, even though you don't love me. I don't know how you do it, I guess it's all those years of practice. So at the end of the year I'm going to quit. I'm going to look for someone to marry. Someone who loves me. Because I deserve it.'' She was proud that she was able to control the tremor in her voice, and she looked him straight in the eye, as coolly and calmly as she could with her heart racing and her hands shaking.

''No!'' he protested.

''Yes, I've thought it out and I'm giving you plenty of notice. Remember you just said you could find another assistant. Remember that no one's indispensable. And another thing I discovered. I like being married.''

''Good, so do I. Stay married to me.''

''I can't do that.''

He stiffened. His eyes narrowed. ''All right,'' he said. ''I accept your resignation as of the end of the year. Naturally I'll write you a letter of recommendation so you can get another job. Maybe you'd also like a letter of recommendation as a wife so you can get another husband?''

''Please, Ben.''

''Please what? Apologize for asking you to marry me forever? Something I've never done before? Something I swore I'd never do?''

''Please don't be bitter. I'm very flattered you want to

stay married to me, but it won't work. Because we both want something different from marriage. You can't deny it.''

"No, I can't. So what do we do? Shake hands and pretend there's nothing between us?''

"If that's what you want.'' She held out her hand.

He took it and jerked her into his arms, holding her so tightly the breath was squeezed out of her lungs. One hand caught her by the chin and he slanted his lips to kiss her. To kiss her as if it was the last time. To give her something to remember him by.

Emily braced herself for the kiss she knew was coming, but nothing could have prepared her for the assault on her lips. The lack of any hint of tenderness. Instead he kissed her with all the pent-up anger and frustration he'd been holding back. His mouth was hot and demanding. She tried to resist. She thought she could, but in the end she met every one of his kisses with one of her own. As if she knew, too, that this was the end. When she finally pushed him away, with both hands on his chest, he turned and left the room without a word, and she went to her room, collapsed on her bed, dizzy, disoriented, with hot helpless tears pouring down her cheeks.

She wondered how she'd ever had the strength to say no when he asked her to stay married to him. It must have been the knowledge that he'd break her heart if she did. She was just lucky he hadn't already done it.

She sat on the edge of her bed and tore open her mail. A bill from the nursery. And a letter from her parents saying they were being audited by the IRS. Emily's tears fell on the handwritten words. On their pleas for help in locating old check stubs and records. Now she'd have to go and help them. Now she'd have to confess she was married and explain why she hadn't told them. On the other hand, it would give her a good excuse to escape from Ben. She'd stay a few days, get things in order and then come back and face the music.

The next day Emily left early in the morning. She placed a note for Ben on the dining room table, explaining why she had to go, packed her bag and tiptoed out of the apartment, fearing every minute that he'd appear and try to talk her out of it. She knew what he'd say. Don't leave now. I can't spare you now. She didn't want to argue with him. She didn't even want to see him. She only hoped that a change of scene would help her cope. Give her the strength to make it through the year as she'd promised. His bitter words rang in her ears.

Maybe you'd also like a letter of recommendation as a wife....

In the taxi on the way to the airport, she was filled with regret. Regret that she'd ever agreed to marry him in the first place. But there was one thing she was proud of. That she'd kept her real feelings from him. That he'd never guessed that she loved him. Loved him more now than ever. Loved the way he looked in the morning after a shower, loved the way he glanced at her across the breakfast table, the way he confided in her. About everything. Not just business, but his family, as well. That Sunday morning he'd brought her breakfast in bed, the burnt toast and the weak coffee. All the moments she would spend the rest of her life trying to forget.

She didn't call her family at the airport when she landed. She grabbed the shuttle, then took a cab to the sprawling old house on the outskirts of Portland. She wanted to surprise them and she wanted a little more time to think up a story. Because she knew what they'd ask. Why was she wearing a huge diamond wedding ring? And so forth.

She was right. Her sister Helen saw her taxi from the window and let out a shout. They came running out to the curb, yanked her suitcase out of her hand and shrieked and hugged her.

"She came. She's here," Helen said.

"I don't believe this," Robin said.

"Why didn't you call from the airport?" her father asked.

"What have you done to yourself?" her brother Paul asked, his mouth open wide.

She shook her head and brushed aside the question. The answer would take hours. What had Ben done to her was more to the point. She realized that while she'd undergone a transformation, they hadn't changed a bit. They continued hurling questions at her, everyone talking at once as they dragged her into the house. She hadn't realized how much she'd missed them. Her father put the coffeepot on, her sister Helen admired her haircut. Her mother, seeing the way the diamond on her finger caught the light, took her hand to look at her ring. If only she'd been able to take it off, she could have kept quiet about the marriage, but unfortunately the ring still wouldn't budge.

The whole family clustered around the round oak table in the kitchen and listened while she told an abbreviated version of the story. Marriage of convenience. Her boss. Her job. A necessity. Not a word about love.

"Your boss, the sheik? You're married to a sheik?" Robin asked. "And you never told us?"

She explained over and over that it wasn't a real marriage, that it would be over in less than a year, but they didn't want to believe that. They wanted to believe in forever after. They wanted to believe in palaces and crowns and romance and love that lasted a lifetime. Emily could understand that. She wanted to believe in it, too. But she couldn't.

Then it was their turn. To tell about the plays they were rehearsing, the auditions, the classes. They would have gone on all day, acting out scenes, telling stories, if she hadn't insisted on going down to the basement and searching through shoe boxes for receipts and records so she could start working on their taxes.

Then she took a tour of the garden. Not surprisingly it needed weeding and not surprisingly she changed into her old shorts and halter top and located her tools from the shed and started digging. She felt needed, wanted and loved. And she felt different. Older, wiser and a little sadder. After dinner her mother took her aside in the yard where the same hardy roses she'd planted years ago still stubbornly sprawled against the fence.

"About this marriage of convenience..." her mother began, taking a seat under the old elm tree.

Emily picked a yellow rose from a dwarf bush. "Yes?"

"Tell me more about your...husband."

Emily only meant to say that he was her boss and that she was doing him a favor, but the sympathy in her mother's eyes, the warmth of her voice tempted her to break her silence, to confess everything. Her unrequited love, her determination to leave him at the end of the year. But she didn't need to. Her mother's intuition made it unnecessary.

"You love him, don't you?" she asked.

Her eyes filled with tears. Was it that obvious? Had anyone else guessed her secret? His parents? His cousins? Or what was worse, had Ben himself guessed?

"Oh, Mom, what am I going to do?" she asked, taking the chair next to her mother and burying her head in her hands.

"Are you sure he doesn't love you?"

"Positive. He doesn't believe in love."

Her mother nodded sympathetically. "That's the worst kind. When they fall, they really fall."

Emily looked up and gave her mother a watery smile. "He's not going to fall. At least not for me. Maybe someone else. Maybe when he finds the right person. I'm not that person."

Her mother gave her a long, knowing look and kissed her cheek. "My dear, darling daughter. Just because you're the smartest one in the family doesn't mean you're not lovable and beautiful, too. In this noisy competitive family it's sometimes hard to know who you are. You had to leave to find your true self and your true worth. I dare say this man, this sheik, had something to do with it. Because you're a different person from the girl who left home four years ago. You're a woman. A lovely woman."

Emily's eyes filled with tears, and her mother deftly changed the subject. From Emily and her secret love the conversation turned to the subject of men in general, and women, and love and marriage until Emily yawned, kissed her mother goodnight and went up to her old room in the attic where she slept soundly for the first time in weeks.

She was glad to be home. Glad to be back among old familiar surroundings. In the midst of her family. Her family who treated her differently than they ever had. It might have been the ring, it might have been her "new look." She realized Ben's condo wasn't home to her and never would be, even if she'd agreed to spend the rest of her life with him, in a loveless, one-sided marriage.

She didn't miss the strain of trying to avoid running into him in the hall or the kitchen after work and on weekends, but she missed other things. The smell of the strong arabica coffee he made every morning, the sight of his dark hair, damp from the shower, his casual clothes that molded to his broad shoulders and muscular legs. The newspaper stories he read aloud to her across the breakfast table as she ate a hasty bowl of cereal before they went to the office together.

With Emily gone, Ben left the office early every day. He found it more and more difficult to work without her. Each day it got worse. He couldn't find anything. He forgot meetings. It wasn't just that she knew where everything was, that she had his schedule memorized. It was that he was distracted, thinking about her night and day.

He realized how much he relied on her in every facet of his business, not just on her knowledge, but on her opinions and her intuition, too. But that wasn't the worst part. Now she'd become a part of his home life. There was nowhere he could go to escape her presence. He picked up the phone a dozen times to call her, to ask her when she was coming back, to ask her how things were going. To tell her how much he missed her. But he was afraid she didn't miss him. He was afraid she'd say she was never coming back. Why didn't she tell him she was going away instead of leaving that curt note? Why didn't she wake him and say goodbye? Why wouldn't she stay married to him?

She was the most stubborn woman he'd ever met. And the meanest. How did she think he'd feel finding her gone that morning? Finding only a brief note? He thought he knew her. He thought he understood her. He thought she'd be thrilled to continue their marriage indefinitely. Forever. Till death parted them. But she wasn't thrilled. She acted as if he'd insulted her.

One day he walked aimlessly down Montgomery Street, turned on Third and marched to China Basin. On the waterfront he stopped and stared at the boats in the harbor.

The memories of sailing with her on their honeymoon came rushing back—the way she handled the tiller despite her lack of experience, the way she didn't complain when she got hit on the head and soaked with icy water. They'd sailed again on the Arabian Gulf at his parents' home. He remembered how the wind blew her hair across her face, how her skin turned golden brown under sun.

That was the problem. The boats reminded him of Emily. Roses reminded him of Emily. Everything reminded him of Emily. It was driving him crazy. Because even though she'd come back when she'd finished at her parents' house, he was afraid she'd still stubbornly refuse to stay married to him, no matter how hard he'd try to convince her. And he'd have to see her every day, at home and at work, knowing it would all end in less than a year. She'd pack up her belongings from his condo, clear out her desk and work and then what? She'd walk out of his life forever.

Never again would he hear her soft voice, never see her subtle curves under her terry cloth robe or her sweet smile at the breakfast table. He never knew loneliness until she left him. Imagine how lonely he was going to be after a year of marriage. He couldn't take it anymore. He had to do something. But what? She wouldn't marry him unless he loved her, and he didn't love her. He'd know it if he loved her, wouldn't he?

His cousin's words came back to haunt him. *You're in love all right. You should see yourself, following her everywhere with your eyes. As much in love with her as she is with you.* Ridiculous. So he followed her with his eyes. So his voice was different when he talked about her. Did that mean he was in love with her? If he was, he was in deep trouble, because she wasn't in love with him.

All he knew for sure was that he was miserable. He hadn't been able to sleep or eat since she left, and it was her fault. His apartment was an empty shell without her. How dare she leave him alone in that hollow mausoleum. He couldn't even work. He'd sit at his desk staring out the window until he had to get up and leave. He'd accomplished nothing since she left. It was all her fault. Why didn't she call him? Ask him how he was doing? How things were going at work?

He spent the rest of the day wandering the streets, heading up the hill toward Pacific Heights. He stopped at Lafayette Park and pulled out his cell phone. He just happened to have her parents' phone number in his pocket. But no one answered, though she said they'd be working on their tax returns. But it was just as well she didn't answer, because he didn't know what to say to her. He kept trying, anyway. He wondered if she'd gone elsewhere. Maybe she'd never gone there at all. Maybe it was a lie. Emily lie to him? Impossible.

He didn't know where he was going. Or why. He caught a cable car and rode it down to the wharf, where he passed crowds of tourists eating ice-cream cones and take-out shrimp cocktails, shivering in their shorts and sandals in the cool San Francisco summer air. Husbands and wives, families with children vacationing together. Fathers carrying children on their shoulders. Mothers pushing babies in strollers. He used to be glad he didn't have a wife hanging on his arm or a crying child.

Now, the sight of these families made him feel inexplicably lonely. He used to be proud of his independence. Now his independence weighed on him like a heavy barrel of crude oil.

He thought of Emily holding his cousin's baby, of the look on her face of pure longing. He remembered her playing croquet with his little cousins. And he knew she'd be a wonderful mother. She was a wonderful wife. His wife.

But not for long. How could she refuse his offer when she knew how he wanted her, needed her. He wanted her so much because he...he loved her. Could this be love, this terrible, awful hollow feeling in the pit of his stomach? This yearning, this longing for something...someone. That someone was Emily. Yes, he loved her. He always thought love, if there was such a thing, would make you feel like dancing, like shouting, like laughing. He didn't feel that way. He felt desperate, edgy, enervated. And what if she didn't believe him when he told her he loved her? What if she didn't care? What if she didn't love him?

He took a taxi to the airport. He was going to find her and he was going to get some answers to his questions. And he wasn't coming back without them.

It was cloudy and overcast in Portland. He took a taxi to the address on the card in his pocket. He stood there in the warm, humid air staring at the large old house. A young woman came walking down the front steps holding a book in her hands.

"'Out, out damned spot,'" she said.

He cleared his throat.

"Oh, sorry. I didn't mean you. Looking for someone?"

"Emily Claybourne."

She nodded. "You must be the sheik. I told her you'd come after her."

He gave her a grim smile. "What did she say?"

"She said I didn't know you. She said you were stubborn and you didn't believe in love. Is that true?" she asked incredulously.

"The stubborn part is," he admitted. "The other part...I've changed my mind."

"Congratulations. I knew you would. Emily's in the garden." She pointed toward the rear of the house. "No surprise there."

He walked around the house past newly planted rose-bushes and opened the gate. It creaked, but she didn't hear it. She was on her knees in front of an old gnarled bush. His heart stopped beating for a split second while he stood in the shadow of the trellis.

"Emily."

Her head snapped up and her jaw dropped. "Ben, what on earth are you doing here?" She got to her feet and stood staring at him for a long moment. He strode across the lawn and faced her.

"I came to talk to you," he said. "Do you have a minute?"

"You came all the way to Portland to talk to me?" she asked. "You could have phoned."

"No, I couldn't." He took a trowel out of her hand and set it on the glass surface of the small table.

"About our marriage..." he said.

"I know what you're going to say. You like being married. It makes you feel good, like a part of the family," she said. "But—"

"But that's not enough," he said. "Not enough reason to get married, or stay married. You said you want to marry someone who loves you. I understand that. Because I want the same thing. You've made a believer out of me. It's taken almost two months, but I believe in love. I've seen what love can do. I, too, want to find someone who loves me, who loves me even when I'm stressed-out, tired, over-bearing, stubborn, obnoxious..."

She choked on a laugh. "Well, that shouldn't be too hard. In spite of your many faults you're not altogether unlovable," she said primly.

"Thank you, Emily," he said with a wry smile. "You should know. You know me better than anyone. You've seen me in all my moods. You even married me when you didn't love me, didn't you?''

"Did I what, love you? Of course not." Her voice shook just slightly on the lie as she leaned forward to pluck a drooping rose from a low bush.

There was a long silence. The perfume from the roses filled the air. He took her hand and pulled her toward the wrought iron bench on the grass and sat down next to her. He tilted her chin with his thumb and forced her to meet his gaze. His dark, penetrating gaze that looked right into her soul.

Emily's pulse raced. He knew. She could see it in his eyes and hear it in his voice. There was no point in hiding it any longer.

"I have a confession to make," she said, averting her gaze. "I did love you. I married you because I loved you and I wanted to help you out."

"Wait a minute. You did love me. But do you still love me? Just a little…Emily?" His voice dropped, his thumb traced the outline of her cheek.

She tried to speak, to say something, to deny it if she could, but he kissed her, heated kisses that scorched her lips, then less frantic, tender kisses that she couldn't resist. She sighed a ragged sigh, laced her arms around his neck and kissed him back.

"Is that a yes?" he asked, moving his lips to murmur in her ear.

Her throat was clogged with tears. She didn't want to tell him. She didn't want him to know. Her most sacred secret. But she managed to say it. "Yes, I still love you, Ben." She buried her face in his chest, and he held her so tightly she could hear his heart pounding. "I always will. But that doesn't mean anything. It doesn't change anything."

"Emily, my darling, it changes everything. I'm such a fool. Don't you know I've loved you from the start? From the day you promised to love, honor and obey me in front of the whole world. And I kissed you. It was then that I knew I was in love with you, had been in love with you for years. I just didn't recognize it. It's taken me so long. So damned long."

She looked up at him, her eyes wide, her lips parted.

"You don't believe me, do you?" he asked. "I don't blame you. Well, I'm going to spend the rest of my life proving it to you. We're going to take another honeymoon to an island and sail and ride and make love in the same bed every night. And then we're going to sell the condo and move outside the city where we can raise roses and children. We'll make a sunken garden, and I'll collect wild birds like Mr. Butchart, a parrot that repeats 'I love you Emily' all day long and I'll—"

She pressed her fingers against his lips. "Stop, Ben, stop. You don't have to do all that. You don't have to do anything. You just have to...love me."

And he did. Forever.

*   *   *   *   *

If you enjoyed what you just read,
then we've got an offer you can't resist!

Take 2 bestselling
love stories FREE!
Plus get a FREE surprise gift!

Clip this page and mail it to Silhouette Reader Service™

IN U.S.A.	IN CANADA
3010 Walden Ave.	P.O. Box 609
P.O. Box 1867	Fort Erie, Ontario
Buffalo, N.Y. 14240-1867	L2A 5X3

YES! Please send me 2 free Silhouette Romance® novels and my free surprise gift. Then send me 6 brand-new novels every month, which I will receive months before they're available in stores. In the U.S.A., bill me at the bargain price of $2.90 plus 25¢ delivery per book and applicable sales tax, if any*. In Canada, bill me at the bargain price of $3.25 plus 25¢ delivery per book and applicable taxes**. That's the complete price and a savings of over 10% off the cover prices—what a great deal! I understand that accepting the 2 free books and gift places me under no obligation ever to buy any books. I can always return a shipment and cancel at any time. Even if I never buy another book from Silhouette, the 2 free books and gift are mine to keep forever. So why not take us up on our invitation. You'll be glad you did!

215 SEN CNE7
315 SEN CNE9

Name	(PLEASE PRINT)	
Address	Apt.#	
City	State/Prov.	Zip/Postal Code

* Terms and prices subject to change without notice. Sales tax applicable in N.Y.
** Canadian residents will be charged applicable provincial taxes and GST.
  All orders subject to approval. Offer limited to one per household.
  ® are registered trademarks of Harlequin Enterprises Limited.

SROM99   ©1998 Harlequin Enterprises Limited

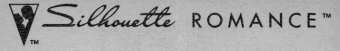

Sometimes families are made in the most unexpected ways!

Don't miss this heartwarming new series from
Silhouette Special Edition®, Silhouette Romance®
and popular author

DIANA WHITNEY

Every time matchmaking lawyer
Clementine Allister St. Ives brings a couple
together, it's for the children...
and sure to bring romance!

August 1999
I NOW PRONOUNCE YOU MOM & DAD
Silhouette Special Edition #1261
Ex-lovers Powell Greer and Lydia Farnsworth knew *nothing*
about babies, but Clementine said they needed to learn—fast!

September 1999
A DAD OF HIS OWN
Silhouette Romance #1392
When Clementine helped little Bobby find his father, Nick Purcell
appeared on the doorstep. Trouble was, Nick wasn't Bobby's dad!

October 1999
THE FATHERHOOD FACTOR
Silhouette Special Edition #1276
Deirdre O'Connor's temporary assignment from Clementine
involved her handsome new neighbor, Ethan Devlin—and
adorable twin toddlers!

Available at your favorite retail outlet.

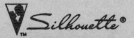

THE FORTUNES OF TEXAS

*Membership in this family has its privileges
...and its price.
But what a fortune can't buy,
a true-bred Texas love is sure to bring!*

Coming in October 1999...

The Baby Pursuit

by

LAURIE PAIGE

When the newest Fortune heir was kidnapped, the
prominent family turned to Devin Kincaid to find the
missing baby. The dedicated FBI agent never expected
his investigation might lead him to the altar with
society princess Vanessa Fortune....

THE FORTUNES OF TEXAS continues with
Expecting... In Texas by **Marie Ferrarella,**
available in November 1999 from
Silhouette Books.

Available at your favorite retail outlet.

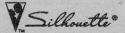

Of all the unforgettable families created by
#1 *New York Times* bestselling author

NORA ROBERTS

the Donovans are the most extraordinary. For, along with
their irresistible appeal, they've inherited some rather
remarkable gifts from their Celtic ancestors.

Coming in November 1999

THE DONOVAN LEGACY

3 full-length novels in one special volume:

CAPTIVATED: Hardheaded skeptic Nash Kirkland has *always*
kept his feelings in check, until he falls under the bewitching
spell of mysterious Morgana Donovan.

ENTRANCED: Desperate to find a missing child, detective
Mary Ellen Sutherland dubiously enlists beguiling
Sebastian Donovan's aid and discovers his uncommon abilities
include a talent for seduction.

CHARMED: Enigmatic healer Anastasia Donovan would do
anything to save the life of handsome Boone Sawyer's
daughter, even if it means revealing her secret to the man
who'd stolen her heart.

Also in November 1999 from Silhouette Intimate Moments

ENCHANTED

Lovely, guileless Rowan Murray is drawn to darkly enigmatic
Liam Donovan with a power she's never imagined possible. But
before Liam can give Rowan his love, he must first reveal to
her his incredible secret.

Silhouette®

Available at your favorite retail outlet.

Look us up on-line at: http://www.romance.net

PSNRDLR